Conversations with Mademoiselle ZoZo

Evelyn De Wolfe

"Conversations with Mademoiselle ZoZo"

By Evelyn De Wolfe

Copyright © 2010
ISBN 1439268444
First Edition

Published
by
The Ashlin Press
Hollywood, California

Layout by GT Litho
Printed In the United States of America

Copies of this book may be ordered
by contacting the author at
evie2000@dslextreme.com

Preface

The story of ZoZo reminds us that the value of a doll is not measured by how much it costs but what it means to a child, and what it means to the doll collector, historian and costumer in endless fascination.

The author spins an enchanting tale about the adventures of a cherished Grödnertal doll (c. 1810) and shares with the reader her journey of discovery as she recreates life in rural France in the early 19th century, and records the fashion trends (1800-1850) reflected in the ever-changing wardrobe of Mademoiselle ZoZo.

I like this book . It deserves a place on any doll fancier's bookshelf.

Karen Rockwell,
President
United Federation of Doll Clubs

iii

Il ne faut jamais mentir, Mademoiselle,
c'est fort mal ! Pour votre peine, vous allez
avoir le fouet !

Introduction

While exploring the back alleys of a flea market in Paris, I came across a small leather-bound book written at the turn of the 19th century. It would become the inspiration for "Conversations with Mademoiselle ZoZo."

In the French novelette Madame de Renneville described the adventures and misfortunes of a doll named ZoZo and gave a fleeting glimpse into French family life during the post-Revolutionary period. It was apparent the author hoped to teach as well entertain her young readers, warning them of the consequences of bad behavior, a lack of education and disregard for moral values.

It brought to mind the unique role that dolls have played throughout history in introducing girls and boys to the complexities and demands of a grown-up world. Flipping through its pages it was easy to reach back to my own childhood and identify with young children who often cling to a favorite object for companionship and reassurance. Mine was a small Steiff monkey which I cherish to this day.

Whether a stuffed animal, a frayed blanket, a toy

soldier or a doll, the cherished object becomes the trusted friend, the playmate -- a sort of talisman endowed with supernatural powers. Together in the confines of a child's fantasy world, they rule kingdoms, travel by magic carpet, mimic the adults and sort out the angels from the dragons that govern their lives.

It was a happy coincidence that our study group, made up of doll collectors and costumers had scheduled a visit to the *Chateau de la Poupée* in the outskirts of Lyon, where enchanting vignettes portray the interaction of 19th century children and their toys.

There I proudly showed my purchase to Michel Gablin, a young Frenchman in charge of the museum's animated displays.

"What a rare find," he exclaimed, "You have come all this way to make us jealous," he added, charmed by the old gravures in the tiny book yet puzzled by the author's reference to the doll being made in Lyon. "In earlier days dolls and doll parts were largely imported from Germany and then adapted to our French taste," he commented.

Still focused on the doll's provenance while visiting the ancient quarters of Vieux Lyon, I stopped by the *Librairie Ancienne Clagahe* and asked the bookseller if he had any information on doll making in that region.

"We do have one major work that lists every trade in Lyon since its earliest commerce. Let us see what we find," offered the amiable shop owner, Monsieur Van Eecloo, clearing his desktop to make room for the massive *Dictionnaire des Artistes et Ouvriers d'Art de la France (Volume Lyonnais)* by Marius Audin and Eugene Vial (1918).

Turning to the index, he quickly ran a finger up and down the listings and after a brief pause, shook his head. "Sorry Madame, I find no mention of doll makers in Lyon."

"Could dolls have been made by puppeteers?" I suggested, knowing that Lyon was famous not only for its silk industry but also its puppetry.

Monsieur Van Eecloo again obliged and rechecked the index. This time he searched under various headings, *pouponnier, fantoche, marionette...* and suddenly his face lit up. "*Voilà!* It states here that puppeteers occasionally occupied themselves with the making of dolls in wood or carton."

Our quest had provided a delightful diversion ... though by now it hardly mattered whether the doll had been made in Lyon or elsewhere. Infinitely more intriguing to me were the conversations a child might have had with her doll two centuries ago.

What followed was a compelling desire to indulge my imagination by retelling the old French tale in my own fashion, within an historical framework hoping to add to the modern reader's understanding of the social and political changes affecting French family life during the first half of the 19th century.

"Conversations with Mademoiselle ZoZo" is divided into two segments:

PART I (Zozo's Story) is a series of separate episodes describing the doll's adventures while living with each of several young mistresses.

PART II (The Way It Was) shares my note-taking on this journey of discovery. It offers a medley of historical data; innovations ensuing from the Industrial Revolution, a "profile" of Mademoiselle ZoZo, and an overview of Parisian styles from the early to mid-1800s as reflected in the doll's ever-changing attire.

The doll featured in "Conversations with Mademoiselle ZoZo" is a beautifully preserved 200-year-old "wooden" in my personal collection and a recipient of two Blue Ribbon awards from the United Federation of Doll Clubs.

Evelyn De Wolfe

Part I

The ZoZo Story

La petite fille

CHAPTER
One

The Belmonts

Paris, France, in the early nineteenth century was not the city modern tourists have come to know. There were no broad boulevards or a star of avenues radiating from the Arc de Triomphe. There was no Moulin Rouge or Folies Bergère, and not even the Eiffel Tower. Those more modern unforgettable images only came into being during the Second Empire, after Napoleon III commissioned a radical transformation of the Parisian landscape.

Our story goes back to when France was mostly rural; when the Arc de Triomphe stood alone in a wooded area at the gates of the city and the city's major landmarks were the ancient Notre Dame cathedral, the Louvre, the Palais des Tuileries with its magnificent gardens, and the Champs -Élysées, then a fashionable promenade of footpaths, fountains, and gas lights.

Paris was embroiled in a maze of narrow, ancient cobbled streets and filthy alleys, yet burgeoning with monumental aspirations and literary giants such as

Balzac and Victor Hugo, and a dynamic spirit engaged in intense land development, in its flourishing industries and the arts. Paris had also become the world's undisputed arbiter of high fashion.

Claude and Yvette Belmont were part of the region's affluent elite. As the eldest son of post-Revolution bourgeoisie, Monsieur Belmont inherited sole proprietorship of two thriving textile mills that could barely meet the demand for the new intricate and highly prized designs from its Jacquard looms.

The Belmonts and their five-year-old daughter Mimi lived in the outskirts of Paris, in a three-story chateau overlooking the Seine Valley. It was near a small park with stone benches, a small fountain, flowers and nicely trimmed hedges where Mimi and her nanny Jeannette took their morning walks.

The estate was largely furnished in the angular, painted surfaces of the transitional Directoire style that flourished after the reign of Louis XVI, and displayed an impressive collection of Sèvres porcelain. It was amply staffed with house servants, a caretaker, a stable boy and a coachman for each of two carriages available to family members.

Mimi, an only child, was taught to do what was

expected of a young member of "polite" society. She tried hard to please her parents, almost never forgetting to say please or thank you, or watch her table manners, or pick her clothes off the floor. Though she did slip up occasionally.

Yvette Belmont was quite pleased with her daughter's efforts and one day took Mimi aside and told her she would reward her for good behavior, with something she'd kept hidden in her bedroom for quite some time.

"What is it Mama that you have hidden from me?"

"A little friend to keep you company."

Mimi's dark blue eyes glistened as her mother reached for a large box on the very top shelf of her armoire. Then seeing the look of expectation on her child's face, Madame Belmont purposely heightened that moment of suspense by taking her time in untying the bright red ribbon that fastened the lid to the box.

"Oh, do hurry, Mama," the child pleaded. "Pleeease?"

Inside the large box were countless items tucked away in tufts of tissue paper, and in the very center lay a wooden doll with delicate jointed limbs... her upswept hair held by a small gilded tuck comb, her pierced ears adorned with tiny emerald drops and her lovely face framed in wispy ringlets.

"Voilà chérie! Meet Mademoiselle ZoZo," exclaimed her mother, handing the doll to Mimi. "She can stand and sit, and move her little arms and legs. She's also very wise, and may even teach you a thing or two."

"Oh, mama, I will love my new little friend."

"Someday I may even tell you her story."

"Does Mademoiselle ZoZo have a story?"

"Oh, yes. Mademoiselle ZoZo has had nine little mistresses before you and many, many adventures. You must take very good care of her so that someday another lucky little girl may enjoy having her."

"Oh, Mama, I promise to take good care of her. And if she misbehaves, I will be cross with her and punish her but I will never stop loving her."

Mimi took her new role as the doll's mistress very seriously.

Each morning she would lay out the clothes that ZoZo would be wearing that day, whether for their morning stroll with her nanny Jeannette, or on an outing to the city with her mother.

"Which of these pretty dresses does Mademoiselle

ZoZo wish to wear today?" Mimi would ask her doll.

"All of them."

"All of them? You're being silly, ZoZo. Don't you know you can only wear one dress at a time?

"But I like them all."

There were so many pretty clothes to choose from. ZoZo had lived with several wealthy families and had always been dressed in the latest fashion. She also had her own little bed, an armoire, two trunks filled with dresses, petticoats, slippers, bonnets and accessories. She even owned a silver tea service, but that was not all. ZoZo had a bookcase for her tiny books and a desk of black ebonized wood with ormolu fittings.

Mimi spent hours chatting with her doll about things they'd seen or overheard, and ZoZo never seemed to be short of things to say to Mimi. Before long they'd become inseparable companions.

On rainy days Mimi and her doll would sit by a window and watch the raindrops trickle down the glass pane and they would beg the sun to shine so they could go outside and play.

"I don't think the sun can hear us," a little voice would say.

"Why not? Do you think he's asleep?" -

"The sun only sleeps at night."

"How do you know that, ZoZo?"

"I just know it."

There were times when Mimi just couldn't get to sleep and she'd take her doll from her little bed and lay her down beside her, and they would talk and talk.

"Do you remember when Papa took us to the fair to watch the hot-air balloons?

"I do, I do. It was so much fun. There were so many balloons, and lots and lots of music, and lots and lots of people."

"The balloons were sooo-o big and in all those pretty colors. They looked like pieces cut out of the rainbow floating in the sky."

"I think they looked like giant pears carrying baskets filled with people. And the people looked even tinier than me. Hee- hee."

"Do you remember that funny woman?"

"What funny woman?"

"The woman in the striped dress and the straw hat that kept jumping up and down in the basket and waving at us?"

"She looked like a petite marionette."

"ZoZo, someday I want to go up in a balloon."

"Me too, and if I do I'll tell the balloon man to take me to the top of the sky, so I can touch a little star!"

"Let's ask Papa to take us to the fair again, Maybe he'll buy us some more of those bonbons like he did the last time --the ones in the lacy paper cones."

"I liked the ones with the pink filling."

"I liked the chocolate ones."

On and on the dialogues would continue, day in and day out.

Sometimes Mimi would mimic her mother in a lilting voice, praising ZoZo for learning something new or reprimanding her for spilling soup on her dress. Still, the best time of day was when Madame Belmont herself would do the talking. She was a good storyteller.

Often, following her afternoon nap, Mimi would grab ZoZo in one hand and her sewing basket in the other and rush to the sun room adjoining the parlor, hoping to find her mother there.

The sun room was Madame Belmont's favorite place. It was filled with plants and cane furniture. Sometimes she would sit there and embroider or she would set up her easel and paint, or simply water the plants and take in the warmth of the sun that filtered through the ceiling-to-floor windows.

When Madame Belmont was ready to tell a story,

Mimi would curl up beside her on the settee with ZoZo close by, in her own little chair. Half-way through her story-telling Madame Belmont would reach for the silver bell on the side table and give it a few good shakes. Almost immediately Francine, the skinny parlor maid with the missing tooth, would appear carrying a tray with tea, tiny fruit tarts and refreshments.

"Mama, when will you tell me ZoZo's story?" Mimi would ask repeatedly.

"Be patient my child. ZoZo's story is quite long. It has to be told little by little… but not before you complete your embroidery sampler with all the stitches I taught you.

"Look Mama, I finished them all," exclaimed the little girl, taking the sampler from her sewing basket and handing it to her mother. "I did the cross-stitch, the shadow stitch, the feather stitch, and the chain stitch. Look, look, Mama…I even did the eyelet flowers you taught me."

"Well done, Mimi. Tomorrow we shall begin ZoZo's story and I'll start by telling you about Eugenie, her first mistress.

CHAPTER
Two

A Special Gift

ZoZo was fast asleep under the pink covers of her little bed when Mimi came rushing into the room, eyes sparkling and her light brown hair bouncing with excitement.

"Wake up, ZoZo, wake up, wake up! We must get dressed."

ZoZo didn't budge. She was much too comfortable resting on her soft pink pillow.

"Didn't you hear me ZoZo?" snapped Mimi, shaking her doll by the shoulders. "We must get dressed. Mama is waiting to take us to the park.

"The park?"

"Yes, the park. Do you know what else she's going to do?"

"What?" moaned the doll.

"She's going to tell us a story … your story, ZoZo."

"My story? But I'm sleepy."

"Oh, do hurry, Mama's waiting."

"I'm still sleepy."

"I'll dress you in your pretty blue gown and you can wear your straw bonnet with the yellow flowers. Now get up, you sleepy head."

It was a short walk to the park. The early morning sun shone brightly through the trees as Mimi skipped along waving to the butterflies that fluttered about kissing the flowers along the hedges. "I'm going to catch one and take it home with me."

"You'll never, never catch it," said the little voice close by.

"Why not, ZoZo?" said Mimi.

"Because it'll flap its wee wings, and fly away. That's why."

"Well? I can move quickly and catch it."

"Oh, no you can't. It'll fly away wherever it wants to go."

"I'll catch the pretty blue one someday, you'll see. And I'll build a golden cage for it."

"Well, that's nice but she won't like it."

"Why not? If I put pretty flowers all around it, the

little butterfly will be very happy."

Madame Belmont soon found a shady spot. She unfolded the quilt she had brought with her and spread it on the ground under the large chestnut tree. And then she waited until Mimi and ZoZo had settled down before beginning the story about the doll's first mistress.

There once lived a merchant in the beautiful town of Lyon, where the wide and sparkling waters of the Saône and the Rhône rivers come together. Lyon is where the finest silks of France are woven, began Madame Belmont.

The merchant, Monsieur Chasson, was a good man and a law-abiding citizen. However, at that time there was a rebellion of the *canuts,* and the good merchant ended up in prison for a crime he didn't commit.

"Are the ca... noots the bad people, Mama?" asked Mimi.

"No, Mimi, the *canuts* are the silk laborers of Lyon. They felt they were not being paid enough for their long hours of labor and so they decided to fight the local merchants. That caused a lot of confusion and many people were blamed for things they didn't do," explained the mother.

Monsieur Chasson's family tried very hard to free him but there was little they could do, except to wait until his case was brought to trial. They were told it could take a very long time and the merchant's six-year old daughter, Eugenie, was heartbroken.

No longer would her beloved Papa run with her across the lavender-scented fields lifting her kite into the windy skies. No longer would he patiently teach her new board games on rainy days, and no longer would he take her to the Sunday puppet show in the main square, and giggle and laugh with her at the antics of the puppet Guignol.

The prison where Monsieur Chasson was being held was a bleak, overcrowded, vermin-ridden building not far from the ancient cathedral of Saint-Jean. It was not a pleasant place for anyone to be in, least of all a young child. But each day, without fail, Eugenie would try to visit her Papa and the jailers found it hard to resist the little girl with the soulful brown eyes and curly hair.

When it happened that Eugenie was denied entry to the prison, she would wait for the right moment to duck under the arms of those waiting in line. At the first opportunity she would run as fast as her little legs would carry her along the dark, damp, stone-paved passageways of the old prison, in search of her father.

Sometimes she would find him half asleep on a straw mat behind the bars of his dreary cell, unshaven, disheveled and underfed; but whenever his loving daughter came to see him, he always managed to greet her with a bright smile.

"Look, Papa, what I brought you," she would say, digging into her apron pocket.

His face would brighten up: "And what have you brought me this time?"

"Some of cook's fresh bread and a slice of cheese."

There were times when she could only catch a glimpse of her Papa in the prison yard. He would be seated in a circle with other inmates reeling out the long, fine silk fiber from the cocoons that would later be sent to the silk spinners and weavers of La Croix-Rousse.

"What is a co…coon, Mama?" interrupted Mimi.

"It is a tiny oval-shaped house that the silkworm builds as its shelter. It produces a fine silk thread that it winds and winds around itself." explained Madame Belmont. "That single thread is so long, it could stretch from here as far as … yes, as far as Avignon."

"That's a very long thread."

"Yes it is, and do you have any idea how many cocoons it takes to make just one of my silk dresses?"

"No, Mama."

"Just think. It takes hundreds and hundreds of them, maybe even thousands and thousands."

No one knew when Monsieur Chasson's fate would be decided, but Eugenie never lost hope and tried to cheer him up by gathering bits of town gossip to entertain him.

"You must thank your Mama for the letters she has sent me," he told her one morning. "Is she better of her broken leg?"

"She hobbles around a bit and hopes to visit you soon, Papa."

"That's good. And what other news do you have for me today?"

"The servants are very upset, Papa."

"They are? Why?"

"I heard Giselle and the other servants shaking their heads and mumbling: "What a pity, what a pity. Poor Josephine."

"What are they upset about?"

"They say Empress Josephine was a good wife to Napoleon and helped him become an emperor. Now he has left her to marry Marie Louise, the daughter of the Austrian emperor. Why would he do that to the Empress Josephine, Papa?"

"Well, perhaps Napoleon had good reason. After all, an emperor needs an heir and Josephine could not give him one. Perhaps the Empress Marie Louise can. Perhaps it's all for the best, my child. You shouldn't be worrying about such things. Now, what else do you have to tell me?"

"Cousin Pierre told Mama about a new invention he read about in the Gazette–a tin can to keep food in. He said that after you put food in it and seal it, it won't spoil for a long, long time."

"Well, I'm sure that will interest your Mama."

"He also told us about the English Fish. He read about that too."

"What English Fish?"

"Not the kind of fish you eat, Papa," she giggled. "Cousin Pierre said that a young poet named Byron crossed the Hellespont waters of Greece swimming as well as a fish. It was a very dangerous and daring thing to do. Now they call him the English Fish. I wouldn't want to be called a fish, would you Papa?"

"Hardly, *ma petite.*"

Weeks and months went by and still no date had been set for Monsieur Chasson's trial, yet Eugenie faithfully visited her father at every opportunity. She was a blessed sight to him and the other prisoners for whom she often ran errands and delivered messages.

Before long, word of the young girl's remarkable devotion to her father and kindness to other convicts spread across the town, eventually reaching the ears of Madame la Princesse, a wealthy aristocrat who lived in a splendid chateau on the slopes of the Fourvière.

Deeply impressed by what she heard, the grand lady decided to use her considerable influence to have Eugenie's father released. But most of all, she wished to reward his devoted young daughter with a special gift.

"Was my doll ZoZo that special gift, Mama?"

"She was indeed, and Madame La Princesse spared no expense in preparing her special gift. The doll arrived with a beautiful trousseau created in the latest Parisian style, along with her little armoire, two trunks, a carved

walnut bed, and a desk. This lady wanted ZoZo to be every bit as elegant as herself, and even ordered jewelry to fit the doll and tiny hankies embroidered with the letter Z".

When the time came to deliver the gift to Eugenie, Madame La Princesse took her aside. "There is something I want you to know," she said.

"My family has a proud heritage. We managed to survive the darkest days of our nation when our king and queen were beheaded by the guillotine. But I want you to know that Mademoiselle ZoZo, your little doll, also has a special heritage".

Eugenie listened. her eyes filled with wonder. "She does, Madame?"

"Most certainly she does *ma petite*. She was born to a tall and mighty tree and shaped into a beautiful doll by the best woodcarver in the Bavarian village of Oberammergau. Even as a small branch she survived the blinding rains and howling winds and learned from the mighty tree, never to despair. Not for one moment. She knew that no matter how harsh a season she might have to encounter, a milder one would surely follow. Mademoiselle ZoZo is very wise and can teach you many things."

Somewhat in awe, Eugenie cradled the doll gently

in her arms. "Oh, Madame, I have never received anything so beautiful in all my life."

What a happy little girl Eugenie had become; she wanted ZoZo to share in everything she did, and now that her Papa had been released, they would once again fly her kite in the lavender-scented fields and giggle and laugh at the antics of the puppet Guignol.

Whenever Eugenie went shopping with ZoZo, the townspeople gathered to admire her, for no one had ever seen such finery lavished on a single doll. Sometimes ZoZo would show up in a morning dress of *bombazine* and a lovely lace cap framing her pretty face. Another day she'd be dressed in an elegant *pelisse* buttoned down the front, over a gown of white lawn. And on warmer days one might see her in a blue striped gown with matching bonnet and a petite parasol.

"ZoZo was the best-dressed doll in the world, wasn't she Mama?"interrupted Mimi.

"She still is, don't you think?" agreed Madame Belmont, "But remember what Madame La Princesse told Eugenie about your doll. ZoZo is not only pretty and stylish; she is also very, very wise."

CHAPTER
Three

Crowns on Their Heads

Madame Belmont grabbed her shawl and wrapped it around Mimi's shoulders. "It's cold and you're shivering, my poor child. I've asked Michel to stoke the fire in the parlor. We can sit there where it'll be nice and warm."

"And will you tell me another story about ZoZo?"

"I will, but first get me the green coverlet that is on my *chaise longue*. And I'm sure you'll want to bring ZoZo with you, as well."

"Oh yes, Mama. She likes listening to your stories."

When all three were comfortably seated by the fire, Madame Belmont began her story. "Unfortunately Eugenie Chasson, ZoZo's first mistress, wasn't able to keep her doll for very long after her father was released from prison."

"But why, Mama?"

"Because Monsieur Chasson's enemies wanted to

23

harm him and destroy his business. He suffered more out of prison than if he'd stayed there. Finally he had no other recourse but to leave the country with his family."

"Why couldn't Eugenie take ZoZo with her?"

"The family had to leave in a big hurry and could only take a few necessary things. They simply had no room for ZoZo and all her belongings."

"I could never, never leave ZoZo," said Mimi, grabbing her doll's tiny hand and holding it tightly.

"We can't always have everything we want, Mimi," whispered the little voice. *"Don't you know that?"*

"Well, Mimi," continued her mother, "If your Papa and I were in great danger, like Monsieur and Madame Chasson, wouldn't you want to do what was best for us?"

"Tell her yes," urged ZoZo.

Mimi was silent for a moment. "Yes I would Mama, even if you were not in danger. I love you so much, and Papa too."

"I know you do, *chérie*."

Mimi looked back at her doll. "You were not happy to leave Eugenie either, were you?"

"I'm sure she wasn't," replied the mother, "but ZoZo soon became accustomed to her new home near Paris where she went to live with her second mistress,

Marie Lavisse."

Marie was Eugenie's cousin – a delightful seven-year-old girl with wavy brown hair, a freckled face and an impish smile. Her parents adored her, especially her Papa who was eager to give her the finest education. He often told his wife: "Marie is as smart as any son we might have had."

At age three Marie was reading small cards printed with the letters of the alphabet and in no time she could spell most words in common usage. At four she spoke French quite well and soon learned some mythology, geography, poetry and general history.

Monsieur Lavisse had been in the service of Napoleon Bonaparte even before he was crowned Emperor of France. He later served in many other important government positions.

Marie's father was a very, very busy man indeed, but he never failed to return home for his midday meal. And if the weather was good he always took his daughter and her doll for a short stroll around their country estate.

"Walking is good for the constitution," he would declare, filling his lungs with the pure air of the woods. On these walks, Monsieur Lavisse would chat about many things that were happening in the nation, as well as in other countries like the United States of America which had close relations with France and which she'd been learning about in her geography book.

Sometimes Monsieur Lavisse would have a copy of the *Journal de Paris* in his pocket and he would read the news to her. He told her about new inventions being welcomed in the wake of the bustling Industrial Revolution, but of all the things they chatted about, Marie had a favorite. It was her father's description of the Coronation of Napoleon I, which Monsieur Lavisse himself attended years before.

He would always begin by saying: "The Coronation took place in December in 1804 -- the very year you were born, Marie. It was cold and snowflakes had been floating down all night long. It made the fields look as if they were covered with globs of whipped cream."

He told her that on that special day, even before dawn, the fireplaces at Chateau Lavisse were glowing, and the Argand lamps were lit throughout the house. Madame Lavisse, who had recently given birth to Marie, was also up early. No one wanted to miss seeing the master of the house in his ceremonial attire.

Everyone was excited and impressed by the fact that Monsieur Lavisse had been personally invited by Napoleon to witness his Coronation. However, all that excitement would soon turn into anxious moments, for an hour had passed and still no sign of Monsieur Lampon, the tailor, and his assistant Perrone.

What could have happened to them? Surely the heavy overnight snowstorm could be blamed for the unfortunate delay but would they arrive in time to deliver Monsieur Lavisse's formal garments?

Finally to everyone's relief, one could hear the faint sounds of a carriage approaching – clop, clop, cloppety clop… clop, clop, cloppety clop growing louder as a pair of horses trudged along the icy road, past the main gate and finally stopping by the side entrance. Two men carrying large boxes stepped down from the coach and were quickly whisked away to the master's dressing chamber.

"What was in the boxes, Mama?" interrupted Mimi.

"Monsieur Lavisse's clothing, of course."

"Did you see them, ZoZo?"

"ZoZo wouldn't know. She was not yet born," reminded Madame Belmont, "Monsieur Lavisse was being suited up for a most important occasion and I can assure you that his garments were made of the finest cloth and sewn to perfection."

He wore black satin breeches, a green double-breasted tail coat with close-fitting sleeves, a gold-embroidered vest, a fob and white neck cloth. Silk stockings and black pumps with silver buckles completed his outfit.

As Monsieur Lavisse was about to leave, his tailor placed a cape over his shoulders and handed him a ceremonial sword and a black bicorn hat topped with a flourish of white ostrich feathers. Dressed *de rigueur* in a tail-coat and powdered wig, Monsieur Lavisse was the image of a true aristocrat.

That day hundreds and hundreds of onlookers stood in the rain to watch the Imperial cavalcade lead a procession of carriages all the way from the Tuileries to the Notre Dame Cathedral where the grand ceremony was about to take place.

Napoleon rode in the royal coach drawn by eight horses and decorated with a large gold letter N. He looked magnificent in his red velvet suit lavishly embroidered with gold thread, and wearing a diamond-studded band across his chest. Napoleon raised his hand to the cheering crowds as they shouted over and over: *"Vive l'Empereur! Vive l'Empereur!"*

"Where was Josephine, Mama?" interrupted Mimi.

"Josephine rode in the royal coach by the side of Napoleon, of course. She was about to be crowned Empress of France. When she stepped from the coach, the crowds went *ooh and aah* for she looked like a fairy princess, sparkling in her beautiful, high-waisted white silk gown encrusted with shimmering jewels."

That night, snug in bed with ZoZo by her side, Mimi could not take her mind off the Coronation and how beautiful it must have been. "I loved that story, didn't you?

" It was like a fairy tale."

Papa said every French child should know about the Coronation because it was the first time France had an Emperor."

"I knew that," chirped ZoZo.

"You're giggling. What are you giggling about?"

"I was thinking about Monsieur Lavisse and his coat tail. Did it wag like Bisou's tail?"

The two were now giggling. "Stop being silly, ZoZo. Bisou is a dog and Monsieur Lavisse's tail didn't wag. It was made of velvet.

"Oh…go to sleep ZoZo!"

CHAPTER
Four

A Mother's Plight

"ZoZo said you didn't finish Marie's story, Mama."

"Oh, did she? Well, the two of you must learn to be patient."

"Yes, Mama."

"As you may remember, Marie was a bright young girl and always studying hard to get good marks from her tutors so she would please her Papa…"

"And she didn't have much time left to play with ZoZo?"

"That's right," whispered the little voice.

"Marie knew she was neglecting ZoZo. She felt guilty that she couldn't play with her as much anymore," said the mother. "She had so much homework."

One day Marie said to ZoZo: "You must be so bored, playing all by yourself most of the time."

ZoZo assured Marie that it was alright. *"We've had lots of good times but you must first please your Papa. He wants you to be a well-educated young lady when you grow up."*

31

"I know that, but it's no fun for you," said Marie.

"Don't worry about me. I know how to play by myself."

"Mama said that my *Tante Giselle* knows of a sweet girl who has no one to play with and is very lonely."

"What's her name?

"Coralie Monchecourt. I'm sure she'd love to have a good friend like you. Would you be her friend?"

"If you want me to," ZoZo replied.

Shortly after, ZoZo was sent to live with her new family in the damp and foggy region of Sologne, in an ancient chateau that looked more like a stone fortress. It had stone towers and even a moat. It wasn't a cheery place at all and Coralie Monchecourt, an only child, most certainly wasn't a happy little girl.

Her father was a wicked man with a dreadful temper. In a fit of anger he had locked his wife in one of the stone towers and forced her to live there alone, with few comforts and hardly anything to eat. But the cruelest thing he did was to separate Madame Monchecourt from their only child.

The six-year-old missed her mother as much as her

mother missed her, but at least Coralie now had ZoZo to share secrets with. In tearful chats with her doll she would tell her: "I can't understand why Papa is so cruel to Mama. I want to tell him how I feel, but I'm so afraid of him."

"You must tell him how you feel." ZoZo would insist. *"I won't let you be afraid."*

Finally one afternoon Coralie gathered enough courage to face her father. With ZoZo firmly tucked under one arm she walked the long, dark hallways all the way to the Grand Hall to wait for him, knowing her father would soon return from a wild boar hunt.

"We'll stand by the old grandfather clock so we can see him when he arrives," she whispered.

"You be sure to tell him how you feel. Just hold me tight and you will not be afraid," assured ZoZo.

"I will. I promise to be brave."

"So stop shaking, Coralie."

The young girl and her doll waited for a very long time before they heard the large oaken door at the entrance groan on its rusty hinges. Monsieur Monchecourt had arrived. He looked so large and so strong and when he slammed the massive door shut, the whole house shook.

Coralie also shook, now more than ever, from the top of her long brown hair to the very tip of her toes. His heavy muddy boots pounded the stone floor in broad, deliberate strides and her large brown eyes widened as she watched her father coming closer and closer.

It was then that he noticed his daughter standing beside the tall grandfather clock in her blue felt slippers and flimsy nightshirt, holding firmly to her doll. He stopped abruptly, towering over Coralie, arms folded across his chest and bulging eyes staring down at her. He looked bigger and meaner than she'd ever seen him.

"What are you doing in the Grand Hall?" he bellowed.

Coralie held ZoZo in a tight squeeze. "Why do you torment my mother and keep me away from her?"she demanded in a firm voice.

"That is no concern of yours, Coralie," he roared back.

"You are no longer my Papa, for I do not wish to be your daughter any longer," blurted the child.

Infuriated by his daughter's impudence, the cruel father snatched ZoZo from Coralie's arms. With a flip of his wrist he tossed her high in the air, so high that the doll landed at the very top of the tall grandfather clock, where the child couldn't possibly reach her. Coralie was now separated, not only from her beloved mother but also from her little friend.

Meanwhile poor ZoZo was left hanging helplessly on the very edge of the tall grandfather clock, with nothing to do but stare at the stone floor below and listen to the monotonous sound of the swinging pendulum marking the passage of time. How long she would have to remain there was anyone's guess.

Despite his wicked ways Monsieur Monchecourt bore some affection for his daughter and fearing she would now despise him even more, decided at last to send her off to her mother.

It was a joyful reunion for Madame Monchecourt and her daughter but it meant that Coralie would also be imprisoned in the tower and would have to survive on little more than bread and water. She had hardly anything to wear or a place to rest except in the frail arms of her mother.

The separation from his daughter soon began to add to the barbarian father's guilt. He hoped to appear less hateful to his child and finally had Zozo brought down from her high perch on the grandfather clock and delivered to Coralie along with other toys.

His gesture had little effect. By then Coralie had become very thin and weak and had little interest in playing with any of the toys, including ZoZo.

Madame Monchecourt knew that idleness and boredom had to be avoided, and did her best to keep her daughter busy with reading and writing. One day she urged Coralie to write a sweet note to her father. "If he reads it, he may give in and remove us from this tomb." But there were never any answers to the letters Coralie wrote.

As the weeks went by the child grew weaker and weaker and one night she awakened from a bad dream with a high fever. Coralie didn't want to frighten her mother with what she had seen in her dream, so she grabbed ZoZo and held her very close. "I saw two executioners enter the tower to kill my Mama," she whispered anxiously. "What are we to do, ZoZo? We must save her."

"We will, we will," said ZoZo.

Madame Monchecourt overheard the terrified child and assured her it was only a nightmare.

"But they want to kill you, Mama" insisted the delirious child, as the worried mother held a wet rag to her daughter's forehead hoping to bring down the alarmingly high fever. There was little else the mother could do except to cradle her daughter in her arms.

After a while the frail child whispered to her mother: "I am dying, Mama," and within minutes she drew her last breath.

Mimi was in tears. "Poor Coralie and poor ZoZo," she sobbed.

Madame Belmont blamed herself for telling such a grim story to so young a child. "I'm sorry this was such a sad story," she said reaching out to comfort her distressed daughter.

"Life can be very hard sometimes, even for young children."

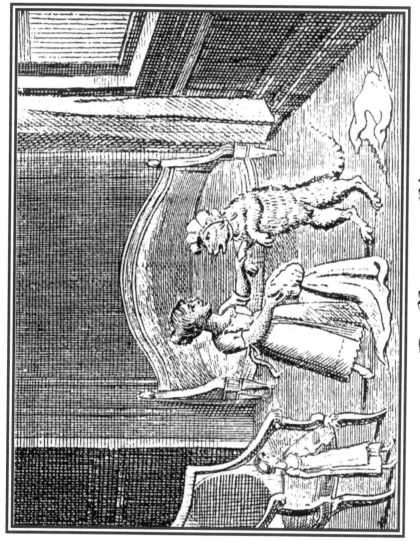

Le Chat coiffé.

CHAPTER
Five

A Topsy-Turvy World

Thus far Mademoiselle ZoZo had lived a fairly normal life among well behaved children, hardly suspecting how quickly that would change. Her world had never been as topsy-turvy as when Fortunée de Villier became her fourth mistress.

Gone were the days when the doll's clothes were tidily put away and kept in good repair. Gone were the days when her bed would be neatly made each day, and gone were the days when she could enjoy some peace and quiet in a well-run household.

"Poor, poor ZoZo," said Mimi, as Madame Belmont began her story.

"Poor, poor me," echoed the small voice nearby.

"France was also topsy-turvy in those days," added Madame Belmont.

"Why, Mama?"

"Emperor Napoleon wanted our nation to be the strongest power in the world but that was not to be. He spent fortunes on his conquests and needed more funds.

He even sold a large part of our North American territory to the young nation of the United States. He was finally forced into exile."

"What is exile, Mama?"

"It is when a ruler is sent to another place and can no longer govern the nation. Napoleon was sent to the island of Elba."

"Was that a jail?"

"Not exactly, Napoleon was a very important person so he was given a personal escort of some 1000 men, a household staff and even the title of Emperor of Elba."

"How long did he have to stay there?" asked Mimi.

"A long time but he managed to escape with the help of his followers and once again he took control of France … but only for one hundred days. After that King Louis XVIII was back on the throne. You will learn more about that later from your history books. Now let's get back to our story.

Fortunée de Villier liked nothing better than to receive presents and when the large package with ZoZo arrived, she couldn't wait to open it. Almost immediately she tore at the wrappings, and shouting with glee lifted ZoZo up in the air and twirled her around and around. "I will teach you to do pirouettes," she laughed.

Before long Fortunée had pulled off ZoZo's hat, rummaged through the neatly folded things in her trunk, meanwhile crushing all her pretty clothes. The way Fortunée was acting, it seemed as though ZoZo herself might soon be destroyed.

"My poor ZoZo," gasped Mimi.

"ZoZo was not having an easy time," said Madame Belmont. "And neither was the cat."

"That's right, that's right," whispered the little voice.

"Did Fortunée have a cat?"

"She had a cat named Minet and she was always trying to dress Minet in ZoZo's clothes."

Mimi turned to her doll. "How awful."

ZoZo rolled her eyes and muttered: *"It's true."*

"Fortunée continued to harass the poor cat, trying hats on her and forcing the poor animal to parade back and forth in different outfits. But one day Minet got really fed up. She had had enough so she jumped on Fortunée and scratched her cheek."

"Bravo, Minet," shouted Mimi, clapping her hands.

41

Fortunée was mean and spoiled and paid very little attention to ZoZo, except when she wanted her doll to take the blame for something she did wrong. "I'll tell Mama that you ripped your beautiful rose dress when we went to Luxembourg and you'll have to stand in the corner with your face to the wall for five hours".

Once Fortunée dropped her dish of blackberry pudding on ZoZo's white pinafore. "Look what you've done. Your dress is all stained. No more sweets for you. Dry bread and water is what we feed to greedy children."

"I'm not like that, am I ZoZo?"

"You're very nice Mimi. I like you," ZoZo whispered back. *"That little girl stamped her feet whenever she was denied something. She also hit her nanny and was disrespectful to her own mother!"*

Monsieur de Villier traveled constantly to distant places and unfortunately was never around to help correct Fortunée's bad behavior. One day his wife received word that her husband had perished at sea.

Madame de Villier was left a large fortune but hardly knew how to manage it. Her attention focused on pleasing her daughter and turning her into a star of society. On day she took Fortunée to Paris to buy her

42

new clothes and while they were there they went to see a show they called the Diorama that all of Paris was talking about. But as usual the spoiled child was unimpressed by everything but herself.

Fortunée did however show some talent for music and dancing at a very young age and Madame de Villier immediately hired the best music and dance tutors to instruct her daughter, while totally neglecting to teach her how to read or write.

Soon the child impressed everyone with how well she could play the pianoforte and how gracefully she could dance the quadrille and the minuet. Encouraged by endless compliments Fortunée was soon in demand as a parlor entertainer.

One day Madame de Villier received a note bearing the royal seal. She was so excited; she couldn't wait to read it. The note was sent by the king's favorite courtesan, the Countess of Cayla, inviting Fortunée to entertain at the court of King Louis XVIII.

Madame de Villier could hardly believe her eyes as she re-read each word written on the blue note paper. She immediately accepted the invitation and quickly hired a specialist in social graces to teach Fortunée the proper court etiquette.

For the next few weeks she fussed over what she and her daughter would wear on this special occasion. She spared no expense and when that day arrived Fortunée looked quite charming in her dainty pantalettes topped by a pink satin frock with puffed sleeves and poufs of lace and tiny roses at the shoulders.

The child performed well and King Louis XVIII seemed quite pleased. After her performance he presented her with a small jeweled box filled with sweets created by Monsieur Debauve, the official *Chocolatier du Roi.*

When it was all over and Fortunée had returned home, ZoZo wanted to hear every detail of Fortunée's visit to the court.

"Did the King like you? Was it all so glittery and wonderful?" asked the doll.

"The King hardly paid any attention to me," grumbled Fortunée. "He never said how well I performed. I performed magnificently. Everyone else said so."

"But he gave you a beautiful box, filled with sweets prepared by the Chocolatier du Roi!"

Fortunée turned up her nose and continued to complain: "Besides the king is disgustingly fat," she added.

"Was the king fat, Mama?"asked Mimi.

"Well, one could say he was somewhat overweight. The king was a *gourmand* who enjoyed large portions of the delicious foods that were brought to his table," observed Madame Belmont. "No one was quite equal to the artistry of the chef at Versailles. But Fortunée should never have spoken about her sovereign in that manner."

Intoxicated by all the compliments received for her daughter's performance at Versailles, Madame de Villier continued to spend far more than she could afford to maintain a grand lifestyle for herself and her daughter.

By the 1820s, the fashion plates in the Parisian journals were showing marked changes in a woman's silhouette -- corsets were being worn once again, the waist was becoming smaller and the slim straight skirts changing to a bell shape, clearing the ground and showing off tiny heelless slippers, many criss-crossed to mid-calf by narrow ribbons.

To Madame de Villier that meant that everything

they wore would have to be modified to keep up with *la mode au courant.* She even insisted on having new clothes made for ZoZo so she would not shame them when seen in their company.

The foolish woman soon squandered most of the fortune her husband had left her by continually buying new clothes, even though the wardrobes throughout the chateau were amply filled with costly costumes.

Eventually, having almost no money left, Madame de Villier could no longer keep up appearances and Fortunée was soon forgotten by those who had previously applauded her. The impoverished mother had to dismiss the servants and sell most of the furniture, but far more humiliating was being forced to take on a modest job as a seamstress. Meanwhile ZoZo and all her things were sold to a rich merchant who bought them for his daughter Celeste.

"I did not like this Fortunée, Mama," said Mimi. "She was vain and didn't know how to do anything except sing and dance. If you needed money like Madame de Villier did, ZoZo and I would hem lots of handkerchiefs for you to sell and you wouldn't have to work."

Madame Belmont smiled and reached for her daughter's hand.

"Let's see… if you and ZoZo hemmed four handkerchiefs each day, in no time at all we would have, let's see…surely enough centimes to see us through."

Céleste et ses Frères.

CHAPTER
Six

The Little Heroine

"Where did ZoZo go after leaving Fortunée?" Mimi asked her mother.

"Don't you remember? A rich merchant purchased her for his daughter Celeste."

"Oh, yes, I remember."

Ten-year-old Celeste Chenault had two younger brothers, Michel and Pierre. She also had a governess named Maxine, who had been with the family ever since Celeste was born.

Maxine taught Celeste many useful skills, and every once in a while she would remind her that: *"Le bon Dieu* gave us hands to help ourselves and feet to walk on our own," and then she would add: "You must be prepared to face any situation."

At the age of six, Celeste already knew how to embroider and braid her own long auburn hair; she could also paint pretty pictures, and as she grew older she enjoyed keeping an eye on her mischievous little brothers whom she swore to protect from all harm.

49

After ZoZo arrived Celeste also behaved like a little mother to her. Every morning she'd ask ZoZo in a stern voice: "Have you washed your face and hands, Mademoiselle?" and at night before she went to sleep, it was always the same question: "Have you said your prayers, Mademoiselle?"

Celeste was determined to teach her doll how to paint. One day she took ZoZo aside and in a mysterious sounding voice announced that she had a surprise for her.

"*A surprise for me? I love surprises,*" said the wee voice.

"Close your eyes then. I'll get it for you."

"*My eyes are closed, my eyes are closed.*"

"You can open them now. Look, it's just your size."

"*My own little easel?*"

"Henri, the gardener, made it for you. He even framed a tiny canvas for you to paint a picture on, like I do."

"*I'm scared.*"

"What are you scared about?"

"*I can't paint.*"

"I'll teach you."

Even though ZoZo had done and seen many

things, she had never experienced anything like painting before. She was so excited.

"When the rain stops and the sun comes out, we'll set our easels side by side under the elm tree and I'll teach you how to paint."

ZoZo and Celeste were both getting impatient because it had been raining for days. And then one morning, after it had been raining for several hours, the sun suddenly burst through the grey mist. Celeste rushed to her room, grabbed ZoZo from her bed and ran to the large window in the atrium

"Look, look, ZoZo!"

"What? Where?"

"Up in the sky. There's a beautiful rainbow. See it?"

ZoZo looked upward into the sky. *"I see it. I see it. It's such a beautiful arc and it's sparkling with colors."*

"Maxine says that if you look carefully at the rainbow you can see every color of everything around us."

"Do you have all those colors in your paint box?"

"Not all of them, but I can make them. Maxine taught me."

"She did? How?"

"I'll get my paint box and I'll show you."

"Maxine says there are three important colors... red, blue and yellow," said Celeste squeezing small lumps of each color on her wooden palette. Now watch me do a little magic, I'll take some blue and mix it with a little yellow. What do you see?"

"I see green ...like the leaves on the trees!"

"Now if I put a little red into the blue, what do I get?"

"Purple ... the color of your Mama's velvet gown."

"You're so smart, ZoZo."

"What does the yellow do?"

"Don't rush me, ZoZo. First I must finish the painting of the fruit bowl I am giving Papa for his birthday. There is one fruit missing. What would you like to see next to the grapes?"

"An orange."

"That will be pretty. Now I can show you what yellow can do when I mix it with a little red," said Celeste, moving her brush back and forth while blending the two colors, then dabbing it on the canvas. Doesn't it look like a real orange?"

"Oh, I want to eat it."

"Well, you can't, silly. It's for Papa."

Maxine often took the children to the fields nearby where the boys would gather poppies and wild flowers for Celeste to weave into garlands. And one day, after some pleading, she agreed to take them on a picnic to a nearby forest some distance from the chateau. The day beckoned and the weather was perfect, as the little group set out on their adventure.

Having reached their destination, they all sat under a large oak tree and enjoyed the delicious country meal that Cook had packed -- bread, cheese, pieces of chicken and an apricot tart.

It was after they finished eating the tart that the sky suddenly turned to a dark grey followed by thunder and bright, scary sparks that flew across the sky. Maxine hurriedly folded the checkered ground cloth and gathered their belongings. They had to find shelter quickly and had barely reached a small cave when the rain came pouring down.

As they watched from their refuge, the rain continued to pour and a strong wind swept through the forest, uprooting several small trees. Then there was silence; the rain had stopped as if someone had suddenly turned off a giant faucet in the sky.

Maxine decided they should quickly make their

way back to the chateau, not realizing how badly the heavy rains had flooded the fields. They looked like a vast sea of mud. Maxine had no choice but to march the children across the watery ground, hardly knowing what they were stepping on.

Maxine carried the eldest boy on her back, while Celeste took the younger one. The young girl protected ZoZo the best way she could by folding her wee arms and legs, wrapping her in a cloth napkin, then dropping her inside her skirt pocket.

ZoZo didn't know what was happening. She remained in the dark, tumbling inside Celeste's skirt pocket and listening to the swishing sound of the water as Maxine and Celeste dragged their feet through the soggy fields. But the worst hurdle was still ahead and soon they would have to cross a deep ravine that had now turned into a small river.

Forging ahead unafraid, Celeste was the first to step bravely into the gully, urging Maxine to follow as they struggled against the rushing waters carrying two very scared little boys on their backs. The young heroine never once lost her composure as she led the little group safely back to her anxious parents at the chateau.

ZoZo remained with the Chenaults for several years after their big adventure, but having no younger sisters to play with her doll Celeste felt it was time to find ZoZo a new mistress.

She chose carefully. She chose Simone, the daughter of the postmaster of Perigueux.

COME SI LEGGE

| d | b | c | d | e | f | g | h | i | j |

| K | l | m | n | o | p | q | r | s | t |

| u | v | x | y | z | ç | é | à | è | ù |

| â | ê | î | ô | û | ë | ï | ü | œ | w |

| , | ; | : | . | ? | ! | ( ) | « | * | » |

SEGNO MAIUSCOLE		SEGNO NUMERI
	LE LETTERE MAIUSCOLE DEVONO ESSERE SEMPRE PRECEDUTE DAL 'SEGNO "MAIUSCOLE"'	
	I NUMERI DEVONO ESSERE SEMPRE PRECEDUTI DAL SEGNO "NUMERI".	

SEGNI MATEMATICI

| : | ∴ | + | − | × | / | = | > | < | √ | (|) | [ ] |

CHAPTER
Seven

The Magic Dots

The postmaster of Perigueux hurried home carrying a large package for his daughter Simone, a six-year-old. He was smiling as he came closer to the cottage where they lived. "Won't she be surprised," he thought even as he unlocked the front door and called out:

"Simone! Come quickly, I have something for you."

"A present for me, Papa?" she screamed with delight.

"Yes indeed, a present for you… but not from me. No, it is sent by Mademoiselle Celeste Chenault, the young lady who comes in every week with her Papa to collect his letters."

"She is giving me a present? But why?"

"I told her how very special you are to me."

Simone lowered her voice, almost to a whisper. "Is that because I am blind, Papa?"

"No, *chérie,* no. But because I told her how

helpful you are to *Grand-mère* … she who can hardly take care of you nowadays."

The postmaster's only child was both sweet and intelligent. He loved her dearly although there was little he'd been able to do about her blindness, except to read to her every evening and teach her simple skills around the house."

"I can't wait to open my present, Papa," exclaimed Simone, clapping her little hands joyfully.

"It's here, on the table."

Knowing its position, Simone walked step by step toward the table and with arms outstretched reached with her fingers across the smooth wooden surface until she could touch the paper wrapped around the package.

"First let me cut the string that binds it," said her father, drawing a small knife from his pocket. Simone waited for the snap of the string, then impatiently tore at the wrappings, gropping through the crushed paper before pulling up her surprise.

"It's a doll, it's a doll Papa! How wonderful!"

"A very pretty one it is and with all her pretty things, as well," he marveled. "I will describe each one to you later, but first let me read the note that is pinned to your doll's dress."

"Oh yes, Papa. Oh, yes, do."

"The note, my dear, is from Mademoiselle Chenault, and this is what she says: 'Dear Simone, your doll's name is ZoZo. She has been my little companion for a long, long time, through thick and thin, but now I'm all grown up and I wish to pass her along as a gift to you. She's very smart and I'm sure she will make you very happy.

"I remember your Papa told me you cannot see, and yet how much you would like to be able to read a book, if that were possible. I thought about my own Papa who knows someone who can teach you. Would you like to meet him? Your friend, Celeste Chenault."

So overwhelmed was the postmaster's little girl that she couldn't speak. But then she could hardly contain herself and in a rush she said: "I would like so much to read, Papa, I would, I would, but how is that possible when I cannot see?"

"Monsieur Chenault told me he would arrange for you to meet a famous teacher of the sightless, who happens to be his good friend ... his name is Monsieur Louis Braille."

The little girl was quiet for a moment, and then blurted out: "Oh, Papa, I do want to meet this Monsieur Bre…"

"Louis Braille."

Weeks went by, until one day the postmaster of Perigueux received an invitation to visit the Chateau Chenault with his daughter so she could meet Monsieur Braille. When that day arrived, Simone was overjoyed.

"I'm going to scrub my cheeks until they look like two shiny apples," she told ZoZo, who stood by while Simone braided her light brown hair.

"What dress are you going to wear?"

"The purple dress with the yellow flowers that *Grand-mère* made for me for my birthday."

"It's so pretty. And don't forget your wooden clogs."

"I won't. Now give me a hug before I go."

Before kissing her grandchild good-bye, the grandmother tied a pretty bow on the lavender ribbon that hung from Simone's straw bonnet. She looked pleased at the way her grandchild looked, and also had a bit of advice.

"We are poor but we are proud," she reminded. Remember Simone, you must be on your best behavior when you meet Mademoiselle Celeste and of course, Monsieur Braille."

After being introduced to the famous teacher of the

blind, Simone tugged at her father's coat sleeve and whispered: "What does he look like?"

"Oh, I would say... of average size, quite slim, quite elegant, with regular features and long looped hair."

Then, in an easy, gentle tone, came the voice of Monsieur Braille: *"Petite Simone,"* he said. "I shall teach you to read many books, if your Papa is willing to bring you for a lesson when I come once a month to play the organ at the cathedral. Now give me your hand," he added, leading her to the settee.

"Still unable to believe what she had just heard, Simone asked excitedly: "But, monsieur how is it possible for me to read when I cannot see?"

"I cannot see either, Simone."

"You cannot see, Monsieur?" she gasped.

"I lost my sight when I was three years old and it took me a long time to find a way to read easily and then teach others to do the same. Can you recite the alphabet, Simone?"

"She knows it very well, Monsieur Braille," interrupted the postmaster. "My daughter has a good mind and some knowledge about many things besides the alphabet."

"Well my young friend, I have created a way for

those of us who cannot see, to recognize every letter of the alphabet with their fingertips. With my system each letter is contained within a group of raised dots. You will be able to identify each letter of the alphabet when you learn the position of its raised dots. When you know that you will be able to join one letter to the other and form a word and then a sentence."

"Will I really be able to do this, Monsieur Braille?"

"Surely. Let's go the desk where I have placed a page from a special book imprinted with raised dots. I will show you how this works," said the teacher, taking Simone's hand and gently guiding her fingers over several small groups of raised dots. "When you come to the end of this sheet, there will be a long raised line. That tells you to turn the page and continue to read more and more."

"Monsieur how did you discover something so wonderful?" marveled Simone.

"I cannot take all the credit. In the time of Napoleon there was a French army captain who gave me the idea for my system. He used raised dots for communication during the many wars, even though the soldiers were not blind. Can you guess why, Simone?"

"No, monsieur."

"Well, it was a way for soldiers on the battlefields to read simple coded messages without their enemies hearing them or knowing where they were, for they did this in the dark... That, however, was not very practical for those who really couldn't see. And so I developed the method that now bears my name –the Braille system."

"Our friend is much too modest," interrupted his friend Monsieur Chenault. "He is a genius and a fine musician as well as an inventor. He plays the organ in churches throughout France and several other instruments equally well. Each month he comes to Perigueux to play the organ in our cathedral. I can arrange to send a carriage to bring you here if Monsieur Braille wishes to teach you."

"It will be my pleasure to teach this young girl, for I can tell she has a quick mind. I have no doubt she will learn quickly."

That very night after Simone returned home, she couldn't wait to tell ZoZo all about her visit to Chateau Chenault.

"Monsieur Braille told me he could teach me how to read."

"How?"

"With magic dots."

"Magic dots? What's that?"

"You'll find out."

"Oh."

Thereafter whenever Monsieur Braille came to Perigueux, a carriage would be sent to bring Simone and her father to the chateau for her lessons. She was a bright and eager student and made amazing progress in the months that followed. Her teacher was both astonished and delighted.

Each day without fail Simone would take ZoZo to her favorite hideaway by a large walnut tree behind the cottage. There they would practice her lessons.

"I want you to learn too," Simone told ZoZo and each day she would take the little doll's wooden hand in her own and run it over the raised groups of letters together, with Simone spelling each word as they progressed.

It was comforting having ZoZo always by her side sharing in her progress, but one day Simone decided that ZoZo was outsmarting her.

"From now on I'm going to blindfold you," she said reaching for a small hankie in her apron pocket and tieing it around ZoZo's forehead...

"Why are you doing that?"

"So you can't cheat," said Simone, wagging her finger.

"I don't cheat,"

"I know that, Mademoiselle. But if you can't see, you won't get ahead of me."

By late summer Simone had become such an excellent reader that her teacher asked the postmaster if he would allow his little girl to help him present his system at the prestigious National Institute for the Blind in Paris. Together they would demonstrate the six-dot method of Braille's invention that was destined to transform and enrich the quality of life of sightless people worldwide.

What an honor, thought the postmaster. What an opportunity to show that even a blind child can be taught to read!

The demonstration was scheduled to take place in Paris in two months, but as the date approached, the postmaster became very worried. He was not a rich man by any means and even with a little help for expenses from Monsieur Braille and the Institute, he would still not be receiving any income while he and Simone were away at the capital.

Simone understood her father's concern and felt it in her heart. She knew how hard it was for her Papa to make ends meet on the little money he made as the postmaster of Perigueux.

"I must find a way to help Papa," she would confide in tearful conversations with her doll. "I must help him."

"I want to help him too."

"Papa says we must go to Paris to help Monsieur Braille.

"You must go."

"But what can I do, ZoZo?"

Suddenly the wee voice within the doll broke the awkward silence:

"I think I can help,"

"You, Mademoiselle?"

"I'm worth something aren't I --with all my beautiful clothes and furniture?"

"What are you trying to say?"

"If your Papa can sell me he will have the money he needs."

"No, no, ZoZo. we can't sell you. You are my friend and the only thing I treasure that is my very own."

"Sometimes we must choose between the things we want and the things we need. We need to help your Papa. We also need to help Monsieur Braille perform the magic of his dots."

"You wouldn't be angry if Papa sold you?"

"No."

In a sudden burst of emotion, with tears rolling down her cheeks, Simone grabbed ZoZo and hugged her. "I will never forget you for wanting to help Papa and me and Monsieur Braille."

Josette

CHAPTER
Eight

Playing With Fire

ZoZo went from living a simple life in the modest home of the postmaster of Perigueux to entirely different surroundings, after Madame de Vertingen purchased the doll for daughter Josette.

Her new family lived in a beautiful chateau south of Paris not far from the vineyards of Burgundy, Champagne and the Loire. Unfortunately for ZoZo, Josette was just as spoiled, demanding, fickle and quick-tempered as Fortunée, who once danced for King Louis XVIII.

This six-year-old climbed on chairs, rolled on the floor, ruined the furniture, soiled her dresses, damaged her toys, yet never once was she scolded. Her mother was enchanted with her and granted her every wish.

When Madame de Vertingen brought ZoZo home, she was neatly wrapped in a package tied with a blue ribbon. As soon as Josette saw it, she pulled off the ribbon and quickly tore into the wrappings. She loved getting presents and couldn't wait to see what new surprise she would get.

When she saw ZoZo she grabbed her by her feet. swung her around with such abandon that the doll slipped from her hand and fell to the floor.

That fall really shook up ZoZo but at the same time she knew that if she were made of porcelain instead of wood she would have broken into hundreds of pieces.

"I'm beginning not to like this little brat," ZoZo mumbled half to herself.

"You must treat your doll more gently," cautioned Josette's mother. "She belonged to a blind girl who took very good care of her. Your doll's name is Mademoiselle ZoZo and isn't she pretty?"

The capricious child shrugged her shoulders and instead of thanking her mother for the gift, all she could say was: "I'm much prettier than she is," and pushed the doll aside with her foot. "Why didn't you buy me a new doll?"

Thereafter Josette rarely played with ZoZo except when she was bored and tried to teach her how to dance. ZoZo did her best to stand up straight and move her little feet and slender legs, but if she so much as tripped, Josette would yell at her.

"You are so clumsy, ZoZo. Why can't you learn a simple step?"

One day Madame de Vertingen surprised her daughter with yet another gift.

"Here's your new doll… just like you wanted," said the mother. "She was made in the workshop of Monsieur Pierre Francois Jumeau, the best doll maker in Paris."

The new doll had delicate features painted on a paper-mache shoulderhead mounted on a kid body. The only features the two dolls had in common were their wooden hands. Josette inspected her new toy from head to toe, tugged at her bonnet and even lifted her doll's skirt to see what was under it. She wore a colorful regional costume from Bretagne that included a striped skirt, a long-sleeved blouse; a green waistcoat decorated with embroidery, a long white apron and starched linen headgear.

"Do you like her?" asked the doting mother.

"Well, at least she's new."

"And what will you call her?"

"I'll call her Joux-Joux."

ZoZo and Joux-Joux soon became close friends since neither doll received much attention from their owner.

"I don't think Josette likes us," said Joux-Joux.

"She's spoiled, that's what she is," replied ZoZo.

Meanwhile Josette blossomed into a lovely looking girl with a graceful figure, rosy cheeks, expressive blue eyes and long dark hair that tumbled softly over her shoulders. But inspite of all these physical attributes Josette was always bored and still had no manners .

She would get up late, change her dress ten times before deciding what to wear. She tormented the cat, irritated the dog, ordered her chamber maid about and angered the servants who had to interrupt their work to act out her fantasies.

This demanding child was repeatedly warned not to get too close to the edge of the pond behind the estate. It was deep and murky but filled with sparkling red fish that could be seen near the water's surface darting back and forth.

So one day Josette decided to take her two dolls to watch her catch a red fish.

"Your Mama said not to go near the pond," said ZoZo.

"She said you could fall in and drown," said Joux-Joux.

"I know what I'm doing. I'm going to catch that fish and I won't fall. I'm too smart to fall in," said Josette impatiently. But wouldn't you know it, Josette did lean over too far trying to catch the red fish and fell into the pond with all her clothes on. She tumbled into the dark and murky water getting both dolls quite wet from her big splash.

"Help, help," shouted Josette as she floundered about in the water, "I can't swim, I can't swim," she shouted, her voice filled with fear and her arms flailing in panic. "Do something, do something. I'm drowning."

Now what could two little dolls do to save her? Not much, even though they tried. Josette was out too far and besides she was much too heavy for them to lift out of the water. They could only wish for a miracle and a miracle did happen.

Just then, Gaston the gardener heard the cries for help and rushed toward the pond. When he saw Josette flailing her arms in the water he kept saying: *mon Dieu, mon Dieu* and reached into pond, pulled her up by her skirts and saved her . He had come just in the nick of time or she would have surely drowned.

When Josette finally got home , drenched and covered with slimy pond scum, she blamed her dolls for making her fall by daring her to catch a fish.

On another occasion after being told never to play with fire, Josette decided to toast some snails and grabbed a hot ember from the kitchen stove. She blew and blew on it until it glowed. But soon the piece of coal became much too hot for her to handle and she dropped it on her dress. In less than a minute the fire spread to her arms and scorched her pretty hair.

To add to these unfortunate happenings Josette's father was suddenly taken ill and died, leaving his inexperienced widow to manage a large estate and a child she could not control.

Burdened by her new responsibilities Madame de Vertingen was also taken ill and soon died leaving Josette an orphan. Fortunately an old aunt was willing to raise the child and it was rumored that the girl was later forced to earn her keep working as a common laborer in the aunt's vineyard.

"I'm sure you want to know what happened to ZoZo and Joux-Joux after Josette was sent to live with the old aunt," said Madame Belmont.

" Well, no one knows what became of Joux-Joux. She simply vanished. Meanwhile ZoZo and her belongings were gathering dust in some dark corner of the chateau.

"Fortunately the housekeeper felt sorry for ZoZo and took her home." said Madame Belmont. "There's more to this story, but I am expected for tea at Marguerite Chopin and must hurry."

"Poor ZoZo!"sighed Mimi, kissing her doll.

"Ups and downs, downs and ups. That's the story of my life".

la Biche blanche

CHAPTER
Nine

The Little Seamstress

ZoZo wasn't very lucky while living with the willful and fickle Josette. No one even noticed that she had been left behind when Madame de Vertigen sold her chateau and dismissed all the servants.

Sophie Berlot, the family's longtime housekeeper was the last to leave. She was on her way out carrying her bundle of clothes when she noticed ZoZo lying in a dark corner by the kitchen.

"You poor little doll," she said, dropping her bundle and placing ZoZo and what remained of her things in an empty carton. "I won't leave you here to be thrown out with the trash, you can be sure of that, little one. I shall take you with me and clean you up. We will soon find you a new mistress."

The kindhearted woman took great care in cleaning ZoZo's delicate face and limbs; she washed and repaired her torn clothes and removed the scratches from her furniture. She then carefully packed the doll with her few belongings and handed her over to Monsieur Brideau, the village baker, as a gift to his daughter Lucile.

ZoZo was happy in her new simple life in the small cottage by the edge of the forest. How different it was from living in the grand style with Josette who neglected her and her other doll Joux-Joux.

Lucile was the very opposite of Josette. She had a good mind and a gentle heart and had learned many practical skills from her parents. At a very young age, Lucile's mother taught her how spin. sew and knit simple things like scarves and socks. And now she couldn't wait to make lots of new clothes for ZoZo.

The clothes that Lucile made for ZoZo were not quite as fancy as the ones she had been used to, but that didn't make a bit of difference to ZoZo. She loved them all the same, especially the little blue-and-white striped pinafore with buttons down the front.

When it was announced that the Brideau family was expecting another child, everyone was overjoyed. Unfortunately Madame Brideau had a difficult childbirth and was confined to her bed after the baby was born. She wasn't even strong enough to attend the christening of baby Michel at the local church. She died soon after leaving Monsieur Brideau and Lucile grief-stricken.

Though barely twelve years of age, Lucile willingly took over the household duties and ZoZo also helped out by keeping baby Michel entertained while Lucile did the chores.

Unfortunately tragedy would strike the Brideau family once again in less than a year. It happened one night during the rainy season as the village baker was returning home from work.

It was misty and the country road leading to the cottage was muddy and slippery. Monsieur Brideau could barely see the road ahead except when an occasional flash of lightning lit up the sky. As he continued on his way home dodging the large mud puddles, he noticed the glimmer of a coach lantern in the distance.

He watched as the carriage came closer and closer, and when it was very, very close he quickly jumped to the side of the road to avoid it. Just then one of the horses stepped into a deep hole and the carriage swerved dangerously out of control, hitting the baker and crushing him against a stone wall.

Monsieur Brideau's injuries were so severe that he

was unable to recover. Within a week he was gone, leaving two young orphans quite alone to fend for themselves. Lucile cried for days and days. She only stopped crying when ZoZo reminded her of her father's parting words.

"Your Papa said you must take care of your baby brother and you must remember the useful things you learned, for they will serve you well. Take your hankie and wipe away your tears."

"You're right ZoZo. I must not waste time crying."

With both parents gone and no relatives to rely on, Lucile had a big task ahead but she was determined to follow her father's wishes.

All that was left to her was the family cottage where she had lived from the day she was born. There was little else except for a few pieces of furniture, some sacks of grain, her mother's spinning wheel, several bolts of homespun fabric and Jolie, the family goat.

Isolated in this rustic setting at the edge of a dense forest, there was no one she could talk to except to her beloved doll. ZoZo had always been a good listener and when Lucile had a difficult decision to make, she knew she could talk it over with ZoZo and end up knowing the right thing to do.

On warm evenings they would sit together by the open window and listen to the night sounds – the owls hooting, the toads croaking, the crickets chirping. They watched as the red foxes darted in and out of the bushes and as the salamander wiggled its way along the path.

"Aren't you afraid of any of the animals that live in the forest?" asked ZoZo.

"Why should I be afraid? They never hurt me, and they know I won't hurt them, though Papa once told me a scary story. It was about a white doe and her three baby deer. He said it should teach me to pay close attention even when I felt I was safe."

"Tell it to me," begged ZoZo.

"Well… there was a white doe that lived not far from here, who was trying to find a safe place for her three baby deer. After looking all over the forest she found a small cave hidden in the rocks. It wasn't too big and it wasn't too small and she fixed it up like a little house. It even had a front door."

"With a lock?" asked ZoZo.

"There was a latch on the inside so you could lock yourself in. Whenever the white doe went out searching for food, she would tell her baby deer to latch the door and never let anyone in except her.

"But how will we know it's you, little mother?" asked the baby deer.

"I'll slip my white paw under the door so you'll know it's me. When anyone knocks on the door you must ask them to show their paw."

One morning shortly after the white doe left the cave; there was a knock on the door. It was the big bad wolf pretending to be their mother.

"I'm home darlings. Unlatch the door."

"Show us your paw," said the young deer and the wolf stuck his paw under the door.

"We won't let you in because your paw isn't white." they said.

The wolf scratched his head and thought about what he could do to get his paws on those tender little deer. He was getting very hungry.

After a while the wolf returned once again to the little cave. He knocked on the door and in the gentlest voice he said: "Open up, my sweet children. This is your mother."

"Show us your paw," said the little deer.

The wolf slid his paw under the door. This time he had wrapped it in a white cloth. The baby deer took a quick look and just as quickly opened the door and let the bad wolf in."

"What happened next?" asked ZoZo anxiously.

"He was a very greedy wolf and ate all three little deer."

"But didn't they see that the paw was of cloth and not of fur?" demanded ZoZo.

"That's what Papa said. If the little deer had paid close attention they would have seen that it wasn't their mother's fur paw and they wouldn't have let the wolf in."

"I don't like to hear sad stories."

"Me too. Let's talk about those chattering birds out there. They go on and on. I wonder what they're talking about. " .

"I know", said ZoZo.

"You do?"

"Sure... I was once a branch of a very large tree. I was high, high up. Lots and lots and lots of birds took a rest on my branch when they got tired of flying. They would sit there and chatter, chatter, chatter until it was time to fly off again".

"What did they talk about, ZoZo?

"Oh, mostly the weather. One time a few of them decided to take a vacation and fly off together.

"Really?"

"They wanted to see what the sea looked like and

get to meet the seabirds. They chattered and chattered about that."

"So what happened?"

"They finally gave up on the idea because they couldn't decide how to get there."

"I think you're teasing me, ZoZo."

One day two farm laborers stopped by the cottage hoping to hire Lucile to watch their herds. She was tempted to accept their offer. She liked the idea of earning a few extra *centimes,* for she had very few provisions left – only four sacks of flour with which to make bread, the wild berries she picked in the woods and milk from their goat Jolie.

It was a hard choice but Lucile thanked the men and told them she could not leave Michel who was now 18-months old and in need of constant attention.

As more time went by, Lucile realized that except for her mother's spinning wheel, a bed, a chair and a table, she would have to sell all the other furnishings in the cottage in order to survive.

With the small amount of money she received for the furnishings, Lucile bought flax and wool fiber and began spinning it into yarn so she could knit stockings and scarves to sell.

ZoZo sat patiently by her side and watched Lucile pedal her spinning wheel, hour after hour, twisting the plant fibers and winding them on the spindle.

Occasionally ZoZo would hold up both arms as stiff as she could, to help Lucile roll the finished yarn into separate balls.

Day in and day out Lucile would spin and then knit, spin and then knit, from dawn until it was time to snuff out the candles. To the villagers who bought her knitted goods, it was a rare and touching sight to see a twelve-year-old able to live in a modest cabin, sustain herself and take care of a young brother as if she were his own mother.

The women in neighboring villages also talked about Lucile among themselves. They admired her spunk and flocked to the small cottage not only to bring her more work but also to have their children meet the resourceful young girl, reminding them that a good character and hard work command respect.

Within a year, Lucile had begun selling a few more of her goods at nearby hamlets but not enough because she always had to keep a watchful eye on her mischievous baby brother. If she could only make enough money she would hire a mature woman to take care of Michel. Then perhaps she could fulfill her dream of opening her own little shop in the village.

One morning while at her spinning wheel, Lucile heard a knock on her door. She glanced through the window and noticed a fancy carriage waiting by the roadside. She quickly opened the door and was surprised to see a tall, elegant lady standing there. She had on a splendid cloak ornamented with braid and wore a charming bonnet with a flourish of ostrich plumes.

"Do come in, Madame," said Lucile nervously tugging at her apron.

"In the village, they call you the Little Seamstress. I'm told you sew and knit very well," said the lady, whose name was Madame Le Clot. "Winter is almost here and I wish to buy several pairs of woolen socks. Show me what you have."

As Lucile gathered as many pairs as she could find, Madame Le Clot noticed ZoZo, seated in her tiny chair with her long slim legs gracefully crossed.

"What about that pretty doll?" asked Madame Le Clot after making her selection of socks. "Will you sell her to me?"

"She is my friend. How can I sell a friend?"

"I will pay you a handsome price."

Lucile was taken back. "I've had offers before but always refused to sell her."

"I will pay you three times as much as the highest offer you've ever had."

"Why do you wish to buy ZoZo?"

"Because she is an aristocrat. I know one when I see one. You wonder why? Because I myself am an aristocrat. Just look at the way she sits and crosses her little legs and how she folds her arms so gracefully on her lap. I have good reason to believe she has seen better times."

"Well...I 'll have to ask Mademoiselle ZoZo what she thinks of your offer. I would like to give her a better life."

The lady smiled. "Of course you must ask her. It would be grossly impolite not to."

Lucile stared at ZoZo hoping to sense her reaction. She moved closer to ZoZo and whispered in her ear. "You've lived in these shabby surroundings for so long. Would you like to go with this nice lady who thinks you are an aristocrat?

"I am quite happy here. It is you who must take her offer."

"Why must I take her offer?

"This is your opportunity to get someone to take care of Michel and to set up your own little shop in the village. You deserve that chance and I want you to accept that offer."

"Don't you think I would miss you terribly?"

"And I'd miss you too but I want the best for you, because I'm your friend."

And so once again our little ZoZo came to the rescue of one of her mistresses, and was ready to move on.

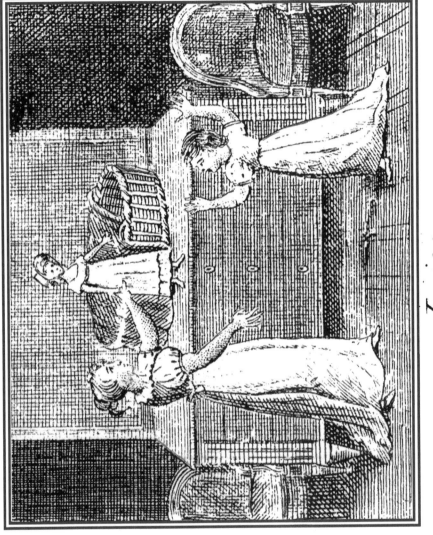

Louisa.

CHAPTER
Ten

The Little Meddler

Mimi sat ZoZo in her chair and crouched down beside her. "No more dawdling, ZoZo," she said, wagging her finger. "We have to practice our lessons. If not, Mama won't tell us another story about you".

"*I already know my story.*"

"You always say that. But let's see how much you know about mythology. Who is Saturn?

"*He's the son of the sky.*"

"And who is Jupiter?"

"*He's the son of Saturn and Cybele.*"

"And who are the brothers and sisters of Jupiter?"

"*That's too many questions,*" grumbled ZoZo.

"Ceres and Junon are his sisters, and Neptune and Pluto, his brothers.

"*Who's Ceres?*"

"She's the goddess of the injured.

"*And who is Neptune?*" continued ZoZo.

"Now stop it, ZoZo. I'm the one asking the questions. So, who is Neptune?"

"The god of the seas, of course."

"Very good, ZoZo. Now we can put away our homework and wait for Mama to return from Paris."

"Why didn't she take us to Paris?"

"Because."

"I think I hear the carriage ..."

Mimi rushed to the kitchen to find Francine. "Is Mama back yet?"

"Not yet, and stop fidgeting, Mimi. And don't nag her to tell you another story. Your Mama will no doubt be tired when she arrives. Today is Wednesday and you know where your Mama goes every Wednesday."

"To the salon of Madame de Malakoff."

"Yes, so don't bother her. She may want to rest."

"Oh, alright," sighed Mimi. Back in her room, she took ZoZo by the hand and walked toward the window. "I don't know why Mama has to go to Madame de Malakoff's salon every Wednesday."

"Don't you know that grownups also have to learn?"

"Yes, but Mama knows a lot already. Why does

she have to learn more?"

"Because she wants to learn more. Your Mama always says that when you stop learning, you stop growing. Don't you know that?"

"But Mama is already grown up."

The carriage had just arrived and Mimi rushed to hug her mother. "You must be very tired, Mama. You must rest. I won't even ask you to tell us a story today…"

"What? No story?" said Madame Belmont, arching her eyebrows

"Well…not if you're too tired."

"I feel quite rested, *chérie*, and quite inspired after listening to Louise Colet's beautiful poetry," said the mother, reaching for another hug. "Have you and ZoZo completed every bit of your homework?"

"Oh yes, Mama."

"Well then, if Francine has our tea ready, I will tell you about Louisa."

"Louisa?"

"Louisa was the last of ZoZo's young mistresses—that is, before she came to live with us.

"It was quite some time since ZoZo had enjoyed the elegant lifestyle to which she had been accustomed," said Madame Belmont. "And you may remember that by the time Lucile sold her doll, ZoZo had practically none of her belongings left. She only had a few of her old dresses and a few simple ones that Lucile made for her. But inspite of everything ZoZo had been through and everything she'd lost, there was something that never changed."

"What never changed, Mama?"

"Her pride, her poise and her infinite patience. Madame Le Clot, the fine lady who purchased ZoZo from the little seamstress recognized those qualities immediately. Remember that she called your doll an aristocrat?" said Madame Belmont.

Madame Le Clot was indeed a lover of the arts and admired the fine talent that went into creating ZoZo. She wanted her restored to perfection. First she took ZoZo to her cabinetmaker for a good polish, then to the best doll costumer in Paris, with special instructions on what outfits to be made for her.

"This is Mademoiselle ZoZo," she told the dressmaker. " I want you to sew a complete trousseau for her.

I don't want her wearing only the Empire style of her earlier days. That is *passé*. She must have at least three new dresses in the latest fashion -- in lawn, taffeta and brocade."

"Permit me, Madame, but *moiré* is also currently quite in fashion. Shall I use it as well?" suggested Mademoiselle DuBois, the costumer.

"Oh, by all means. I also want matching slippers and pretty bonnets for each outfit. And do not forget to make a complete set of underthings -- petticoats, pantalettes, chemisettes, as well as a nightshirt and lace cap. Can you remember it all?"

"Rest assured, Madame, I have a good memory."

"Splendid. Finally we need a long coat, a cashmere shawl, and a party gown."

"Would you like the party dress done in pink silk with an overskirt of tulle, sprinkled with *pailettes*?"

"That would be nice; also make her one in lavender silk with lace trim."

"Will that be all, Madame?"

"Yes, I shall be looking for a few charming accessories on the Rue de la Paix."

After the trousseau had been completed to

Madame Le Clot's satisfaction, she placed ZoZo and her beautiful new trousseau in a large wicker basket, lined in pink taffeta, and festooned with pink silk ribbons. She then took it to the home of her favorite niece, Juliette de Passant.

"What have you there, *Tante Elise,*" Juliette exclaimed on seeing the beautifully decorated basket.

"Louisa will soon be eight years old and I have commissioned a special birthday gift for her. It has required a lot of preparation and I do hope she takes good care of it."

"Dear aunt, you've gone to so much trouble to please Louisa," she marveled, hesitating for a moment before asking her aunt for a favor.

"What favor do you wish from me, Juliette?" asked Madame Le Clot.

"I have good reason for not wanting Louisa to know what's in the basket, not just yet." she said. "I hope you'll let me use this beautiful present to help correct a few of my daughter's shortcomings, most of all her uncontrollable curiosity."

"Do as you wish, my dear. We must always think of ways to teach our children. Prying is not a good trait at all," agreed the aunt.

Juliette de Passant took the basket and made sure it was sealed on all sides so Louisa couldn't possibly peek into it. She then placed it on top of the chest of drawers in her bedroom where it was plainly visible.

As soon as Louisa caught a glimpse of the large decorated basket. she was filled with curiosity. "What is in the basket, Mama? Who sent it? Tell me, Mama. Is it for me? Tell me, tell me?" she fretted.

"In time, in time, my child. Don't keep bothering me about this. I've told you repeatedly that it's impolite to show so much curiosity about everything. Prying is a very bad trait."

"But, Mama..." The poor child was in state of torment.

"I shall not tell you what is inside the basket. Instead I will put you to a test, Louisa. If in three months you are able to correct your excessive curiosity, as well as your other ugly habits, you will be allowed to look into this mysterious basket.

"During those three months I will keep a list of your slip-ups. At the end of that time I will show you my list and judge you accordingly."

"Three months, mama? That's too long," moaned Louisa.

Three months did seem like a long time to test a little girl like Louisa, who had never been able to control her curiosity. It was either a drawer she would open to see what was inside, even in the house of strangers. Or it was a package she might open, without permission. Everything aroused the urge to look inside -- any box, any trunk, even a sealed envelope.

"Sorry my compulsive child, the test cannot be any less than three months for you to learn and for me to judge. In three months from this day you will be allowed to look into the basket ... or it will disappear forever from your sight."

"Without seeing what's inside?"

"That's right. Unless we try this, you will never conquer your unfortunate behavior."

Up until then, reprimands and scolding had had no effect in correcting Louisa's flaws. But even more shocking than the child's craving for looking into things was her incessant prying into every secret that was hidden from her.

The child even put her ear to closed doors to listen

to what went on in other people's lives. When the servants caught her in the act she would beg them not to tell her mother and kept right on doing the very same thing. Louisa was not only extremely curious but a tattle-tale as well. She couldn't hold back any secrets.

"Goodness, what a bad little girl," Mimi cried out in disgust. "You hated her, didn't you ZoZo?"

Madame Belmont reminded her daughter that ZoZo couldn't have witnessed any of this behavior. "How could she hate Louisa when she didn't even know what was going on? ZoZo was sound asleep inside the basket."

Mimi turned to her doll. "I always knew you were a sleepy-head."

Madame de Passant had instructed everyone in the household to report to her whenever Louisa misbehaved. Finally on her own, Louisa made up her mind to do nothing that would deprive her of the pleasure of seeing what was inside the basket. She pleaded with her nanny to help her, so whenever Louisa was tempted to misbehave, the nanny would remind her: "Mademoiselle, have you forgotten the basket?"

In the weeks that followed, Louisa's behavior improved so dramatically that Madame de Passant had practically nothing to write down in her notebook. She was delighted to see such improvement and was now quite convinced that her daughter was not incorrigible, after all.

She reasoned that perhaps three months was too severe a penance for a child of Louisa's disposition, so one morning she called her daughter into her bedroom.

"Two months have passed since this pretty basket has been sitting on my dresser. We've both been so curious to see what's inside, haven't we?"

"You have been curious too, Mama?"

"Yes, curious but also patient enough to wait for the right time. I'm glad you have obeyed my instructions as well as you have."

"I really tried, Mama. I did, I did."

"I know you did, so I've decided to shorten the duration of the test. You may now uncover the basket ..."

"Really, Mama, really?"

"You may but ... on one condition. If you continue to be a little meddler and a tattle-tale as before, I will put everything back in the basket and give it to a more deserving child."

Louisa rushed to hug her mother. "Now can I see what's inside the basket?"

"Of course. Let me help you remove the wrappings, very slowly and very carefully."

Louisa couldn't contain her joy at seeing the wonderful things that emerged from the basket, especially the doll. At that moment she was the happiest little girl in the world.

"What shall I call her?"

"She already has a name. She's Mademoiselle ZoZo."

"Hello Mademoiselle ZoZo. You are so pretty." screamed Louisa.

From that day on, Louisa became a changed child and tried to please her mother in endless ways.

ZoZo liked her new little mistress. She was neither a selfish, curious, nor a misbehaving child. Of course, ZoZo never knew the old Louisa.

When the time came for having tutors, Louisa decided on her own to give up playing with her doll in favor of her studies.

"Then what happened to ZoZo?" asked Mimi.

"It so happens that Juliette de Passant, Louisa's mother, is someone I have known for many years. She is the one who gave me the doll to give to you more than three years ago," explained Madame Belmont.

"You were still too young to play with ZoZo, so I put her away until I felt you were ready to enjoy her and take good care of her. Perhaps someday your own story will be added to those of ZoZo's other mistresses.

"Really, Mama?"

"I do think so, but it will be up to you to decide whether you want to be known as a good little mistress or a bad one. Meanwhile enjoy ZoZo while she is yours!"

The End

Part II

The Way It Was

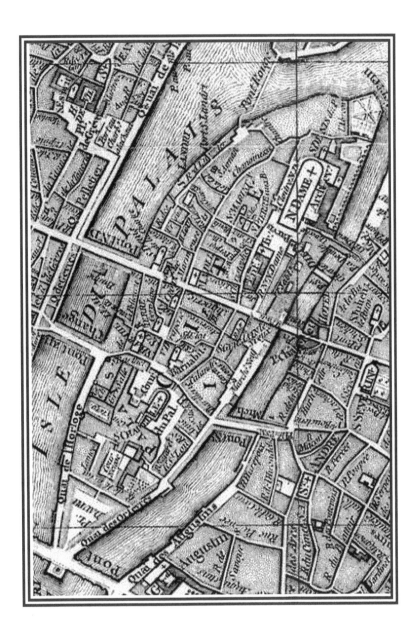

A Bit of History

Our story takes us into the early 19th century when the empire of Napoleon Bonaparte stood at its most impressive and imposing stage.

In this period France was mostly rural and about half of its population did not speak French. A patchwork of dialects kept families pretty much confined to their townships and villages, and those who were wealthy and educated gravitated to the splendor and prestige of the nation's capital.

Paris was the pride of the nation. Its social life was brilliant; its salons stimulating and centered on painters and "literary lions"; the opera was scintillating and the gowns opulent.

When studying early fashion plates we realize how closely variations in fashion relate to what happens in a particular civilization at a given time. Immediately following the French Revolution (1787-1799) styles reflected an aversion to all excesses indulged in by the nobility, and men began adopting the simpler English country fashion. Women reached back to the classical lines of Greek attire, covering themselves with simple chemise-like garments made of lightweight, sheer fabrics gathered at the bust line and sometimes worn over flesh-colored body suits.

Commenting on this period, fashion historian James Laver stated that: "henceforth the classes could no longer be distinguished by striking differences in dress. Yet change in fashion, especially for women, happened

more frequently, since only by adopting the very latest novelty could a woman of wealth distinguish herself from her sisters."

The color white which had been a primary color choice was soon replaced by blues, pinks and crimson and the styles also began to change. The free-flowing neo-Grecian style gave way to a bell-shaped silhouette, and then more changes occurred, namely a return to a natural waistline; skirts became progressively larger with each decade and by the 1850s crinolines and steel cages were needed to support them.

A Fashion Icon

At the start of the new century Empress Josephine was seen as the ultimate trendsetter of fashion. She soon popularized the term "bon genre" (the beautiful people) and promoted glittering functions such as the opera, the masked balls and "soirees" that enabled the elite to parade in their finery and show off the elegance of Parisian fashions. The prima donnas of the Théâtre Français also greatly

influenced *la mode au courant* by what they wore on stage.

Emperor Napoleon fully endorsed his wife's flamboyant efforts and was dedicated to making France a leader of fashion and innovator of design and craft skills, since the country's textile industry had fallen far behind the industrial machinery and textile advancements by the English. To make up for this inequality, the emperor declared an embargo on the import of all English textiles, and focused on reviving the Valenciennes lace industry in France and on improving the manufacture of finer fabrics such as tulle and batiste.

The first Empire lasted ten years (1804-1814) and was marked by the aggressive French domination by Napoleon Bonaparte and the reorganization of the European nations. The emperor's defeat by the British at Trafalgar in 1805, followed by his disastrous invasion of Russia in 1812, marked the beginning of the end for the mighty Corsican.

The Bourbon dynasty was restored following Napoleon's exile in 1814 and Louis XVIII became king (1814-1824). This period known as the Restoration extended to 1830 and saw the French slowly adjusting to major economic changes and to the short reign of King Charles X (1824-1830).

The people's discontent with the new monarch for suspending most of the liberties granted when Louis XVIII occupied the throne, led to the July Revolution, a rebellion that forced the abdication of Charles X and elected Louis Philippe, Duke of Orleans, as King of the French (1830-1848). He was the last king to rule France.

Our story continues through the leadership of Louis Philippe, the Second Republic and ends just prior to the major reconstruction of Paris initiated by Emperor Napoleon III in the 1850s.

A Collector's Find

Mademoiselle ZoZo, the muse for this book is a doll in my collection that has amazingly survived two centuries. I named her after a doll in an old French tale and fantasized about where she had been and what she had seen in the first few decades of her life's journey.

This doll fits into a category commonly referred to as "peg woodens", the majority of which originated in Holland, Germany, and Great Britain.

While we're unable to determine precisely where or when ZoZo was made, a doll with her characteristics is generally identified as a Grödnertal. She has the upswept hairdo, the golden tuck comb and small ringlets framing her delicate face. Her slim elongated limbs are skillfully jointed at the shoulders, elbows, hips and knees, and her torso has a high bust line designed to accommodate the Empire style in vogue when she was made. Also of this early period is her flat orange-painted footwear.

Dolls of this type were produced from the early 1800s to early 1900s, notably in Sonneberg (Thuringia), Oberammergau (Bavaria) and Grödnertal (Tyrol). I liked the lilting sound of Oberammergau and chose it for ZoZo's birthplace.

This Bavarian village is noted for its wood carvings and its yearly Passion Play – a four-century tradition started by the grateful villagers of Oberammergau after being spared the devastating effects of the bubonic plague during the Middle Ages.

Note: A doll similar to our ZoZo (c. 1810) is preserved in the doll collection of the Smithsonian Institution and pictured on page 660 of The Collector's Encyclopedia of Dolls (by Dorothy S., Elizabeth A. and Evelyn J. Coleman).

Images in Part I, reproduced from the French novelette, show an earlier doll type about half the size of a small child. They remind us of the 18th century *poupées de la Rue Saint- Honoré* that fulfilled not only the whims of the French aristocracy but were often sent abroad as fashion envoys.

What People Wore

While living with affluent families, Mademoiselle ZoZo's extensive wardrobe was continually being modified and replenished to keep up with the latest fashion.

The images that follow illustrate the more noticeable style changes in silhouette that occurred from 1800 to the 1850s, as ZoZo was being passed from one young French mistress to another.

Eugenie (1810-1813)

During the First Empire (1804-1814) when ZoZo met her first mistress, Eugenie, women still wore the semi-transparent chemise, cinched under the breasts, except that now skirts flared out in a slightly conical shape and the style was less classical.

The doll's first trousseau ordered in 1810 by Madame La Princesse reflected the Empire style and included a long shawl and mini turban – accessories that became the rage after Napoleon's campaign in Egypt (1798-1801), and never really went out of style for the remainder of the century. There was even certain etiquette in how a lady should drape her shawl.

Empress Josephine is said to have owned several hundred stoles and shawls of fine Kashmir wool and embroidered silks. At the time, a lorgnette also became a must-have accessory, even for a little doll that had no problem with her eyesight.

There was a time when women kept their belongings in pouches concealed in their skirts, but by the end of the 18th century they carried "reticules" – small purses that could be hung from the wrist. These dainty purses were later reserved for evening wear and replaced for daytime by regular handbags in fabric or

leather with metal fastenings.

Fanciful turbans were worn for daytime and evening wear and remained popular for many years. Dolley Madison, First Lady of the United States (1809-1817) was especially fond of wearing jeweled and feathered turbans.

Parisian millinery shops showed a variety of poke bonnets, a style introduced earlier in the century and widely favored. It was embellished with all sorts of ribbons, flowers, fruit and feathers.

Marie (1813-1816)

This period known as the French Restoration (1814-1830) was marked by the return of the monarchy. Louis XVIII was made king and ruled for nine years (1815-1824). Muslin and bombazine were still preferred fabrics, with velvets and satins worn in the evening. The *pelisse* was a daytime favorite -- a sort of overdress shorter than the basic dress and buttoned down the front.

Heeled shoes, popular in the 18th century, were rarely worn in the first half of the 19th century. They had been replaced by highly impractical flat or low-heeled shoes meant to appear dainty and feminine. Usually made of soft leather, cloth or silk, they were lavishly trimmed with bows, buckles or tiny flowers and some were secured to the foot by ribbons criss-crossed from the ankle to the calf.

For most women it was a welcome relief when the half-boot replaced these dainty slippers for outdoor wear.

They were far studier and usually made of leather or cloth to match a lady's costume both in color and texture.

Coralie (1816-1820)

There were only slight fashion changes in this period; skirts still fell straight from a short bodice though wider at the bottom and decorated at the hemline with *rouleaux* (fabric appliqués), or embroidered borders. Net was often worn over colored satin slips.

The *pelisse* and the longer redingote were very much in style, as were the long and narrow shawls and feathered boas worn by women, rich and poor, throughout the century.

Before 1818 the waistline still fell directly under the breasts, but soon after the fashion plates were showing a tightening and lowering of the waistline that continued to drop about an inch every year.

Huge muffs were still popular and head coverings came in various shapes from caps to large and small bonnets daintily decorated.

Fortunée (1820-1824)

Still within the reign of Louis XVIII, women's dresses continued to show a dramatic change in style with a gradual lowering of the waistline to its natural position. Small bustles and ruffled collars  for daytime were  introduced and skirt hems now formed a perfect circle and were decorated with ruffles, pipings, tucks and other enhancements. Sleeves were increasing in size and hats were becoming larger and more elaborate.

Necklines plunged once again and a short corset worn to support and accommodate the new heart-shaped bodice styles. Lace-trimmed pantalettes and wreaths of flowers were widely favored by young ladies.

This was also the era of the "Apollo knot" with long curls piled high on the head and held up with ornamental combs.

118

For awhile the oversized muff had been a favored accessory; a lady could slip all sorts of things into it, even her miniature French poodle. By 1820 these large muffs were no longer in fashion and were replaced by the more practical, smaller, rounded ones.

Women displayed a passion for feathers and polished steel adornments and riding habits with voluminous skirts.

Celeste (1824-1829)

Charles X succeeded Louis XVIII and ruled to the end of the decade, as skirts continued getting wider and sleeves extended from sloping shoulders giving the illusion of a tinier waist. Strict corseting, belts and small bustles, also drew attention to smaller waists.

Bold patterned chintzes and plaids and checks were favorite choices for daytime dresses and were often worn with purses in a matching fabric. From 1816 to 1830 hats were quite spectacular both in size and in the

amount of decorations piled on top to provide better balance for the wider sleeves and skirts..

ZoZo owned several small daytime caps and mini replicas of poke bonnets trimmed with flowers and feathers similar to what her little mistresses and their mothers were wearing. Other head coverings included tiny toques with ribbons and frills and a mini satin turban

with a small jewel and an ostrich feather. From 1816 to 1830 hats were quite spectacular, both in size and in the amount of decorations added to them to enhance the wider brims.

Simone (1829-1831)

This is the start of the Louis Philippe era, when women were wearing the leg-of-mutton sleeves or *gigot* sleeves that ballooned from the shoulders and narrowed at the wrists. These voluminous sleeves and skirts were held up by wicker or horsehair frames. Wide -brimmed hats of leghorn straw were lavishly trimmed with flowers and feathers, ribbons and beads, some veiling and a tiny bird or buckle. Burgundy, purple and especially yellow were favored colors. Footwear was featured in black satin with square toes and worn with silk stockings.

Josette (1831-1836)

With Louis-Philippe at the helm of the nation supported by a wealthy bourgeoisie, we enter a more conservative era with less change in style, except for the increased bulkiness of women's costumes.

Fashion continued obsessed with making the waist appear even smaller. The use of heavier fabrics like brocade on very wide skirts and billowing sleeves added not only to a massive appearance but surely to a lady's discomfort. Stays helped mold the figure and hoop skirts helped support the weight of the gowns.

Lucile (1836-1839)

Still within the July Monarchy, (1830-1848) women's costumes were lowered from ankle-length to floor-length and skirts were being pleated into the waistband of the bodice. The *pelerine*, a cape usually made of fur or lace was usually decorated with lavish trimmings on fabric and draped over leg-of-mutton sleeves, adding to the fascination with width to the silhouette.

The cut and trim of a gown made use of darts intended once again to emphasize the small waist, sometimes accentuated by wearing a wide belt. Corsets were now styled to cup the breasts and shaped by gores that tapered down to a point in front.

Louisa (1839-1845)

A preference for width continued but there were a
few noticeable changes. We still see a lowering of skirts
from ankle-length to floor-length and a change in
headgear – from large hats to bonnets worn close to the
head and tied under the chin looking like coal scuttles.

The parasol and the fan were indispensable. The
latter, aside from its practical use, allowed a woman to
sidestep the restrictions of etiquette by artfully handling
her fan to convey flirtatious messages. One unusual fan
even had a tiny convex mirror on its guard. by which a
lady could demurely survey a ballroom scene before
filling her dance card.

If a woman were to touch the edge of her fan with her fingers, it would mean: "I want to talk to you." If she held the fan to her right cheek, it would mean "yes"; if on the left cheek -- "no."

ZoZo's little treasures included a tiny ivory fan sprinkled with pailettes and one with a pastoral scene painted on silk.

Cartridge pleating was widely used to assemble a costume. It facilitated the gathering of large amounts of fabric to a small waistband, at the back and/ or upper sleeve, without adding bulk to the seam.

By this time skirts had multiple flounces in a tiered effect and tapered toward the waist not to detract from the slim shape of the bodice that now extended over the skirt in a pointed shape.

Mimi (1845-1850s)

During the period when ZoZo came to live with Mimi Belmont, Charles Louis Napoleon Bonaparte was elected president of the Second Republic (1848-1852). Shortly after, following in the footsteps of his uncle Napoleon I, he declared himself Emperor Napoleon II (1852-1870).

The 1850s also welcomed a return to modesty, frailty and gentleness.

At this time it was not unusual for a woman to be wearing five to six petticoats. The hooped petticoats were being replaced by the cage crinoline made of steel—a more practical and less cumbersome way of

supporting the billowing garments.

Gloves were usually elbow length for evening wear but took many forms for daytime and were matched to the color of the gown and shoes.

Women of the privileged classes usually owned at least one *parure* – a boxed set consisting of a necklace with matching brooch, bracelet and earrings set with coral, pearls or other precious gem.

An Amazing Century

Mademoiselle ZoZo lived through the most influential single factor to affect the new 19th century – a flourishing and robust Industrial Revolution that began in England in the mid-18th century and expanded rapidly throughout Europe and America.

An agrarian economy sustained mainly by manual labor was rapidly being replaced by machines, bringing about increased production, lower costs, and widespread riots sparked by mounting unemployment.

In France as elsewhere it leveraged a power shift from noble landowners to urban merchants. We can only imagine what our little doll might have heard or seen during this period of massive changes in every sector, destined to affect the lives of every future generation-- economically, technically, socially and culturally.

New lighting systems and faster transport networks were being developed -- first through canal systems, then the railways. And while the bulk of inventions in this period originated in England, America and Germany, France also made significant contributions. Our research focused on a few that were relevant to our story.

The Sewing Machine

Several attempts failed to create a workable sewing machine before the French tailor Barthelemy Thimonnier invented the first functional model in 1830. His sewing machine used only one thread and a hooked needle that made the same chain stitch used in embroidery.

Thimonnier's invention was seen as a huge threat by a group of 200 fuming Parisian tailors who burned down his garment factory and almost killed him.

The Hot Air Balloon

Balloon rides became immensely popular among Parisians during the 19th century, resulting from the invention of two French brothers -- Joseph and Jacques Montgolfier.

When first demonstrated in 1783, these floating balls that spewed fire overhead terrified the mass of the French people. They were in fact so upset by this novelty that the government sent soldiers to protect the balloons and issued the following statement: "Anyone seeing a globe like the moon in eclipse covered with paper or canvas is informed that it cannot cause any harm and will someday serve society."

The Wonder Weaver

An amazing mechanical loom was invented in 1801 by Joseph-Marie Jacquard that simplified the manufacture of complex patterns on brocade, damask and matelassé.

Jacquard's process relied on stiff pasteboard cards with various patterns of punched holes that programmed the loom for greater control and flexibility of new designs. Jacquard's loom was the first machine to use punch cards and is regarded as a precursor of modern-day computer programming.

Not surprisingly the introduction of these looms also caused widespread opposition against the replacement of people by machines. However, by 1812 there were 11,000 automated looms in use in France.

Affordable Images

Fortunately for costume historians, images of what people actually wore in that earlier century became available when Louis Jacques-Mandé-Daguerre, a professional scene painter for the opera, developed one of the earliest photographic processes.

This new method allowed the middle-class to acquire affordable portraits, and gave Americans the first authenticated image of Abraham Lincoln taken in 1846.

The daguerreotype image was imprinted on a copper sheet with a thin silver mirrored surface and mounted in an airtight case. A glass cover protected the photo from oxidation and finger marks. The invention was first publicly announced in Paris in 1839, and while there were other processes competing for attention, scientific etiquette attributed any discovery to the inventor who first published it.

An episode in Part I refers to the Diorama, an early art form also invented by Daguerre which became hugely popular in Paris in the 1820s. The dioramas were large paintings on transparent linen that created a spectacular effect when lit front and back by combinations of light sources. Daguerre skillfully applied the laws of perspective and other stage devices to give the illusion of constant change and cause figures to miraculously appear and disappear. The diorama concept has been extensively applied to museum exhibits ever since.

Games Children Played

Certain games that children play today were just as popular two centuries ago; some even several centuries ago. We can assume that rolling hoops, shuttlecock, cloth puppets and dolls and spinning tops were among the diversions enjoyed by ZoZo's little mistresses.

Hopscotch has been played in most countries of the world as far back as the 17th century. It is known by different names and played in a variety of ways, more commonly by marking a series of squares on the ground on which the children would hop.

In France one form of the game was called

escargot (snail) and played on a spiral path. Players hopped on one foot to the center of the spiral and back out again. A player marked one square with his or her initials, and from then on could place two feet in that square, while all other players had to hop over it. The game ended when all squares were marked and no one could reach the center; the winner was the player who "owned" the most squares.

Marbles is also a very old game; clay marbles were found in many archaeological digs throughout the world, suggesting that the game was popular with both children and adults several centuries ago and played in a similar manner as today.

Cup-and-Ball, known as *bilboquette* in France, was also an ancient favorite. The object of the game is to swing the wooden ball into the cup, a feat that was not quite as simple as it may seem.

Madame de Renneville

Curious to learn more about the 18th century author who inspired this work, I found only a few biographical references since as a writer Sophie Senneterre de Renneville was known simply as Madame de Renneville.

She was born in 1772 to an affluent family from the town of Caen in Lower Normandy, a region best remembered today as a strategic target during the Allied Invasion of Normandy in 1944.

As a young girl Sophie lived through the madness of the Reign of Terror when the ruling faction during the French Revolution brutally killed all potential enemies, of whatever sex, age, or condition. She was barely twenty-one when Louis XVI and the royal family were removed from Versailles and the King was guillotined, followed months later by the execution of his queen, Marie Antoinette.

After living through these extraordinary events that caused major turmoil for the common people as well as the aristocrats, Madame de Renneville turned to writing to help support her family and became a prolific author of children's books. She died in Paris in 1822.

A Basic
Empire Dress Pattern

This pattern of the doll's original gown was drafted to her measurements. The dress is of lightweight cotton gauze in a simple Empire style featuring a short bodice, low neckline and elbow-length sleeves. The skirt hangs from below the bust line in tiny cartridge pleats, cinched together with a ribbon tied in a bow with long streamers.

ZOZO's MEASUREMENTS

Height: 14 inches

Shoulder Width:	2 3/8 inches	Head size:	5 3/4in
Neck:	2 3/8 in	Arms:	5 1/2 in
Legs:	7 3/8 in	Waist:	4 in
Foot:	1 3/8 in	Hips:	6 _ in

Materials Needed:

1/2 yard of fabric

18 inches of 1/4 inch ribbon

Hooks for closure.

Fabric choices:

Lightweight silks, cotton gauze

in white, pastel shades or tiny prints.

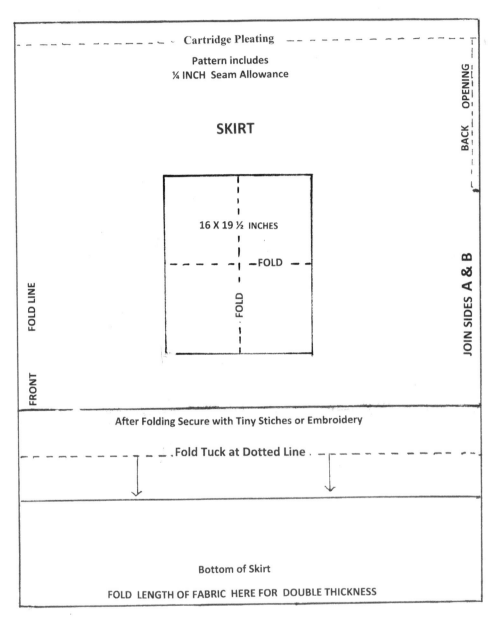

SKIRT

Cartridge Pleating

Pattern includes
¼ INCH Seam Allowance

16 X 19 ½ INCHES

—FOLD —

FOLD

BACK OPENING

JOIN SIDES A & B

FOLD LINE

FRONT

After Folding Secure with Tiny Stiches or Embroidery

Fold Tuck at Dotted Line

Bottom of Skirt

FOLD LENGTH OF FABRIC HERE FOR DOUBLE THICKNESS

Note: Pattern pieces have been reduced by 65%

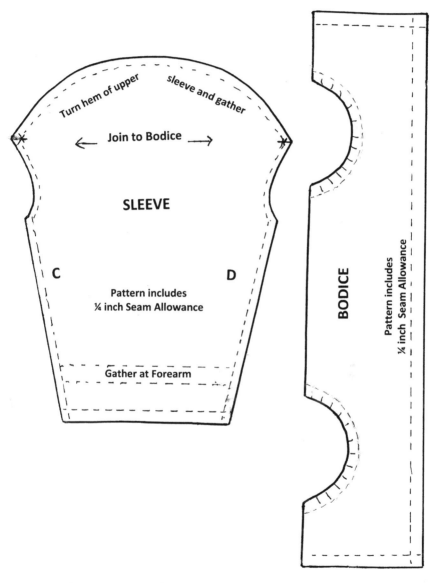

Note: Pattern pieces have been reduced by 65%

Instructions:

1. Cut a piece of fabric 16" long by 19" wide. Fold the square in half . (Folded end will be the bottom of the skirt). Fold again in half, side to side. Place pattern on the 4 layers of fabric and mark accordingly.

2. Make tuck along the entire width by folding on dotted line; place bottom edge of tuck on bottom line at 2 inches from bottom of skirt. Press.

3. Secure top of tuck on dotted line on right side of the garment, using tiny stitches or embroidery. Press.

4. Join sides (A & B) leaving opening at back. (French seam optional).

5. Join skirt to bodice with tiny cartridge pleats, adjusting for proper fit at the bust line.

6. Join each sleeve at C & D

7. Attach sleeves to the bodice by sewing up to top edge of front and back bodice (as indicated). Leave the unattached top portion of the sleeve unhemmed.

8. Hem edges of sleeves and bodice (front and back) and gather all pieces together with tiny stitches, leaving long threads at both ends of the back opening to be tied after gathering to a nice fit around the shoulders.

9. Hem the bottom of both sleeves, and then gather the sleeve a _ inch above the sleeve hem, leaving

loose ends to adjust and secure the gathers just below the elbow.

10. Add embellishments such as embroidery, rosettes, or appliqués to bottom of the skirt and/or neckline and sleeves. Tie a bow with long streamers at the bust line ; if desired repeat ribbon trim on sleeves.

Acknowledgments

I'm deeply indebted to my many friends in the doll world who have enhanced my appreciation for this captivating art form -- in particular fellow members of Heirloom Doll Costumers who so generously share their knowledge at our monthly meetings.

My special thanks to:

Karen Rockwell, collector extraordinaire, for her Preface;

Donna Kaonis, editor of *Antique Doll Collector* for an encouraging review;

Ella Strong Denison Library for permission to use images from its Fashion Plate Collection; Dover Books for consent to reprint sketches from their fashion publications; Wikimedia for access to its public domain images;

Ted Poyser, literary coach, for his on-going support;

Gracie Aldrich, Tatiana Deslandes Mustakos and Milly Blakeley, my young preview readers, for their perceptive comments;

Finally, a salute to authors, too numerous to list, whose painstaking research enriches my own.

About the Author

Photo by Ivo Lopez

Author//journalist Evelyn De Wolfe, a native of Rio de Janeiro, describes her life as an exciting journey. She came to the United States on a student/teacher fellowship, having first served as interpreter for the US Coordinator of Inter-American Affairs and the Office of Strategic Services in her native land.

A graduate of the University of Brazil, her work on war-related projects for the Radio and Motion Picture Division of the State Department in Hollywood led to her being hired by Walt Disney as a story researcher.

She was a member of the Hollywood Foreign Press before engaging in a long career as staff writer and columnist for the Los Angeles Times, later traveling worldwide on free-lance magazine assignments with her late husband, photo-journalist Leonard Nadel.

Her professional credits include a Janus Award for "outstanding reporting" of real estate issues, a merit award from the California judicial system for a series on Crimes Against Children, and a listing in Who's Who of American Women.

She believes one should never fully relinquish the whimsical delights of one's childhood and highly treasures her Honorary Clown & Master of Mirth award from Ringling Bros Barnum and Bailey Circus for her guest appearances as a circus clown.

Comments by Young Readers

"I loved your book. I really loved how the characters were different and had an interesting story behind them. Your vocabulary taught me a lot of words that I could use more often. My favorite character is Mimi. I like how you didn't use plain words. You used exciting words, for example instead of ran you used the word dashed."

Gracie Aldrich (age 10)

"We really enjoyed reading about Zozo's life and her friends and their pets. She lived through lovely times and some very sad ones. Some of her mistresses were heroic, remarkable little girls, while others were selfish, spoiled brats. Zozo lived in luxury and the very opposite sometimes. She learned about history and famous people like Louis Braille, Napoleon, etc. I enjoyed learning about all the little clothes and accessories she was given by each new owner. Zozo's experiences and adventures were great for reading."

Tatiana Mustakos (age 11)
Milly Blakeley (age 5)

Also by the Author:
The Life and Times of Phlange Welder
Across the Herring Pond

31386573R00090

Made in the USA
Lexington, KY
09 April 2014